THE AMBUSH WAS CLOSED FOR LUNCH
And Other Short Stories

By

Nick Brazil

Brazil Productions
Oxfordshire, England

To my dear friends Barbs and Jez with thanks for all their support

First published in 2024
Copyright Nick Brazil 2024
ISBN 9798345387689
Brazil Productions
Whitchurch-on-Thames, Oxfordshire, England

CONTENTS

A Long Tradition 4

The Ambush Was Closed For Lunch 7

The Nabatean Urn 16

The Thirteenth Apostle 29

The Astrologer 49

Nemesis 67

Testiclees 75

The Journey 78

The Robin 80

Bitter August 85

*Report into Special Inspection
of Hogwarts School* 90

The Girl from Saxony 93

The Hunt For La Camargo 110

Mother Lode 117

A Harmless Old Git 129

A Portrait of a Lady 131

Callminder 138

The Man With Healing Hands 143

Flying Forever 144

Escape From Room 101 148

When Boney Invaded Britain 153

A LONG TRADITION

I have always greatly admired the art of short story writing. It is no easy task to tell a whole story with a beginning, middle and satisfactory end in a relatively short number of words. I am sure that the many famous authors from Margaret Attwood to Ernest Hemingway discovered this when writing their own collections of short stories.

Without wishing to put myself in that exalted league, this was certainly my experience when writing the tales in this book. Testament to this is the number of unfinished stories on my files.

These twenty short stories were mostly written sporadically over a period of about twenty years. They were inspired by a wide variety of experiences and memories. Some are based on fact whilst others are pure fiction.

The first story called *The Ambush Was Closed For Lunch* is a true account of my experiences whilst in Albania in 1991. I hope it captures the atmosphere of anarchy, fear and hope in that Balkan country during a chaotic period of its history.

The Nabatean Urn, the next story, is about the consequences of a betrayal of trust and the subsequent theft of a valuable artefact. The acquaintance who related it to me swore it was true. Years later, his widow confirmed the whole story was completely made up. Nevertheless, I am grateful to her late husband for gifting me the material for a very good piece of short fiction. The next story called *The Thirteenth Apostle* is a work of total fiction. The idea of sending someone back in time or in death to resolve a mystery is by no means original. However, I hope that my story gives a new take on this old theme.

The Astrologer which is the next story, is also pure fiction. For the life of me I can not remember what inspired it. I just hope people find this black comedy mildly entertaining. *Nemesis* the supernatural thriller which follows it, was inspired by a visit I and a female friend made to an isolated and ancient chapel high on the misty Lancashire moors. *Testiclees* is a completely true story which I can best describe as a slice of life experience.

The Journey is a flight of imagination and is one of three fictional short stories I wrote with my home village of Whitchurch-on-Thames as the main location.

The Robin is a story whose main character is the author, D.H. Lawrence, with his short stay in Pangbourne, Berkshire, in 1919 as the background. It is based on a letter he wrote at the time. *Bitter August* is an 'alternative history' story with Whitchurch as the location. *Report into Special Inspection of Hogwarts School* is a satirical look at what the school inspectors might think of Harry Potter's Hogwarts. With apologies to J.K. Rowling! The next story, called *The Girl from Saxony,* has an interesting provenance…..

I often have a drink with my good friends Jez and Barbs. One Sunday in late April 2022, Jez told me the dramatic and tragic story of his mother's early life in Germany during and after The Second World War. It inspired me so much that I immediately sat down and wrote this short story based on her experiences.

The Hunt For La Camargo is my very own real life detective story. For many years now I have been trying to locate a beautiful painting which features my grandmother as Marie Camargo a daring eighteenth century French dancer. The only image I have of this painting is a black and white photograph taken when it was exhibited at the Royal West of England Academy in 1910. I think it is one of my best stories and is certainly my favourite.

Mother Lode is a light hearted work of fiction about getting even. Once again, I have no idea where the inspiration for this one comes from. The idea for *A Harmless Old Git* came from a visit to a local barber. This particular man means well, but he really does talk too much. This would not be so bad if he did not patronise his older customers. He assumes anyone who looks a nanosecond over sixty must be spoken to like a four year old child. So, this story is a cautionary tale to show nothing is what it seems. I now go to a Turkish barbers where they speak little or no English.

Portrait of a Lady can best be described as an experimental story based on the life of the American born author Henry James. Although it is written as a work of fiction much of it is factually based. *Callminder* is a fictional story about betrayal and vengeance.

The Man with Healing Hands is my first foray into that relatively new genre of short stories known as flash fiction. As its name suggests, this style of short storytelling uses as few words as possible.

As its name suggests, *Flying Forever* has a strong aviation theme. This is hardly surprising since I wrote it as a tribute to probably the greatest aviatrix who ever lived, Amelia Earhart. However, it is also a story about relationships with a possible supernatural twist. I leave the reader to make up their mind on that score.

Escape From Room 101 imagines how Winston Smith, the main character in George Orwell's dystopian novel 1984, is thrust into modern day Britain. It is a fantasy meant as a tribute to one of our greatest writers.

When Boney Invaded Britain, the final story is an alternative history that imagines what would have happened if Napoleon had invaded the British Isles. Whilst it is a work of fiction of course, I have endeavoured to back it up with as many available facts as possible.

Apart from a few of these stories being published in a village magazine, only one has ever been published in another periodical. This simply highlights the fact that it is increasingly difficult for unknown writers like myself to get their work published anywhere. This is why these stories are seeing the light of day in this self-published book.

I really hope that anyone who reads these tales gets a fraction of the pleasure I had in writing them

Nick Brazil
Whitchurch-on-Thames, Oxfordshire, England
November 2024

THE AMBUSH WAS CLOSED FOR LUNCH

The far corner of the bar at the Pheasant was always the preserve of John Fitzherbert and his little gang of mature drinkers. Any day of the week at early doors you could find John, Harry Darrowby, Bertie Mullins and Cyril Peters holding court and putting the world to rights. As time went on, their numbers decreased, felled by the Dark Reaper's relentless scythe.

Bertie was the first to go. Poor old Bertie, he of the wise word and kind gesture, struck down by a massive heart attack as he washed the dishes. Then Cyril Peters, incapacitated by a stroke that condemned him to a lingering twilight of no speech and little movement. Alone with his many memories he was fed baby food by a wife who had long since ceased loving him. Finally, it was John Fitzherbert's turn. At least his end had been quick. Lifting his first cup of morning coffee, he had a pulmonary embolism and was dead before he hit the kitchen floor.

It was his death that confronted me with the reality and inevitability of my own mortality. *And now I'm the only one left,* I thought. *One moment, I was the youngster of this little band of drinkers and now I am the last old fart standing. How long for?* At seventy-five I was well within The Reaper's sights. Call it superstition if you like, I never sat at that end of the bar. Then along came Covid making it all academic.

It was sometime in the early Autumn of 2021 that I was distracted from these dark thoughts by two friends. Sam and Deirdre Cliff were a couple in their thirties whom I had got to know when they moved into the village a couple of years previously. Some people were a real chore to be with. Not so Sam and Deidre. I have always found their boundless curiosity for all life had to offer a wonderful antidote to my increasingly frequent dark moods.

"Hey Nick, you'll never guess where we've just been," Sam said sitting down opposite me.

"I simply can't imagine."

"Go on give it a shot," Deidre prompted me.

"Oh, I don't know, the Cairo Necropolis?" I guessed.

"Nice try, well presented, but no," Deidre said. "Albania."

"Albania," I said. "A great favourite with Lonely Planet these days."

"You should really give it a go!" Sam said. "Ready for another pint?"

"Yes, same again. Actually, I have," I said, my mind travelling back over thirty years. It was the winter of 1991 and I had been sponsored by the telecoms company I worked for to run basic foodstuffs and medical supplies into Albania for a small charity. The firm had generously loaned me a canary yellow Land Rover Defender 90. *That wouldn't happen these days!* I thought.

Random memories of that chaotic and surreal time crowded in my mind willy-nilly, like a poorly edited documentary. I was back in Puke, that appropriately named poverty stricken mountain town. As our little convoy arrived in the late afternoon, a group of boys and young men who had been wandering aimlessly around the main square clustered eagerly around the Land Rover Defender 90. To my relief, these people were friendly unlike those in some other towns and villages where our aid convoy had been met with a hail of stones.

"Forta Makina! Strong Machine" one man shouted in admiration as he thumped the wing of the Defender with his fist.

After forty years of brutality, squalor and deprivation forced on them by Hoxha's Marxist dictatorship, our arrival in Puke must have seemed like a visit by superior alien beings to the local Albanians. Looking at the sea of grinning faces, I was struck by their gaunt and drawn appearance. This was a permanent legacy of a lack of nutrition.

What our convoy carried were very basic foodstuffs and medicines. Pasta, spaghetti, tinned tomatoes, aspirin and bandages. Those sort of things would not warrant a second glance in Britain, but here, some would even murder for them. As the sun sank behind the jagged mountains dusted with the first snowfall of winter, we offloaded our precious cargo in a secure compound, ringed with barbed wire. If there was one commodity there was no shortage of in nineties Albania it was barbed wire.

We were guarded by a tall, moustachioed man in a thick

brown coat and armed with an ancient, bolt action rifle.

With no artificial lights to cut through the darkness, we had to rely on the trucks' headlamps as we carried the boxes into the storage huts. It was a nocturnal ballet of figures silhouetted against the vehicles' lights. Most of those trucks were from various haulage companies in Britain loaned as acts of charity. One, however, was a local truck, a knackered Soviet Era Skoda with a twisted chassis. It was driven by a relentlessly cheerful man called Stanic. He had been caught by the Sigurimi, Hoxha's secret police, listening to the Beatles and banged up for ten years for his pains. All the more remarkable is that he had no bitterness for this unjust loss of freedom. Stanic lived for the day as he drove his truck swigging from a bottle of local firewater.

After we had offloaded the supplies, my Albanian translator and I spent a bitterly cold night in the cavernous interior of one of the empty HGVs. Curled up in my sleeping bag I hardly slept at all with the nocturnal blackness filled with the sounds of livestock and barking dogs. Albania, I decided, was not a land at peace with itself, particularly at night.

Indeed, driving across that beautiful, chaotic landscape was a dangerous experience both day and night. This was a time when danger came without warning and from the least expected quarters as I would soon discover.

The aid trucks that were flowing in from as far afield as Germany, Denmark and Norway, unwittingly created their own hazards. As they travelled down the main road from the northern frontier at Hani Hotit, the drivers would throw out sweets and bars of chocolate to the children at the side of the road.

Very soon, the kids decided the sweets were not gifts by big-hearted Westerners but an entitlement. On numerous occasions, I narrowly missed running down one of these violent scarecrows as they leapt in front of the Land Rover demanding sweets. When these were not forthcoming, they would hurl stones at the windscreen.

"Why didn't you throw them sweets?" people would ask.

"Because it created a dangerous situation in which those

kids could have been run over and killed. On occasions, they probably were."

"But they were starving weren't they?" was the blank faced metro liberal response.

"And I wasn't St Francis of Assisi or Johnny Appleseed," I would reply angrily. "Look I was there to deliver aid not kill the local population."

My time in Albania, was filled with many striking scenes and memories. One surreal impression that has burned itself on my memory above all others was the thousands of pillboxes littering the mountainous country. On the road to the Northern city of Skhodra, I remember seeing countless domes of pillboxes stretching across unfenced fields. Cows grazed peacefully beside them. Then there was that time in the city of Elbasan in the middle of the country. That was when I came across another of these pillboxes in a children's playground. Its significance was lost on the kids. To them it was just another part of their adventure landscape.

Nobody knows exactly how many pillboxes were constructed on Hoxha's orders. Figures vary from 180,000 to 750,000. What is beyond doubt is that they were a very physical manifestation of the communist regime's paranoia about the outside world. During his forty-one year reign Hoxha told his people they were in imminent danger of invasion by the Americans, British, NATO, Russia and even China, the regime's erstwhile ally. According to him, everyone but everyone was itching to conquer their worker's paradise. The pillboxes were Albania's answer to such aggression.

Mercifully, they were never used. If they had been, with so many nestling between workers flats, hospitals and schools, the civilian casualties would have been truly horrific. Today, with Albania, a military member of NATO, one of Hoxha's chief potential foes, many of his pillboxes have been converted into restaurants and shops by resourceful Albanians.

In the month I was in Albania, I travelled hundreds of miles delivering supplies to hospitals critically short of even the most basic medicines. In one, I recall seeing a nurse changing a nappy by the late afternoon light of a window. She had no option since all the hospital's light bulbs had been stolen. In another, a medicine cabinet contained nothing but a pair of false teeth grinning as if in mockery. Next to the cabinet, two syringes lay on a wooden bench without sterilisation or protective cover.

If I had an accident on one of the country's lethal roads, I would not have fancied my chances either since there were only three working ambulances in the whole country. As Sam and Deidre chatted happily away about the rustic charm of modern Albania, I knew they had no inkling of the squalid and dangerous place it had been so recently.

For example, there was the *Sigurimi,* the secret police, whose members had a healthy distrust, not to say hatred for aid agencies and do-gooders like me. As far as they were concerned, we were Western spies and foreign interlopers. Whilst much of this was driven by xenophobia, it was also because foreign aid workers made the Albanian Government look bad. This was because NGOs were supplying food and basic necessities to the local population which the authorities had signally failed to do.

Whilst the former communist, now "social democratic" government officially welcomed the foreign aid agencies and their workers, its secret police worked hard to obstruct and intimidate them.

On one occasion, I was driving the Land Rover in a two-vehicle convoy with a small red Talbot car in front. We were travelling towards Bajram Curri, a notorious bandit town in the northern mountains. The Talbot was being driven by an Italian-Albanian called Pierrino. Somehow, he had been left behind when his parents split up, and his Italian mum returned to her native Italy.

This had left him a sorrowful prisoner of Marxist Albania forever longing for Italy and his mother's cooking. Employment as a driver for our little charity proved to be a godsend. Pierrino hoped they might even wangle his passage to Free Europe. The dream of democracy might have come to Albania, but Pierrino suspected this was just a mirage with Hoxha's heirs waiting in the shadows to return to power.

Pierrino mistook my smattering of Italian for total fluency and would conduct long conversations with me in his native language. It did not matter that I hardly understood any of it; I liked him all the same, and he was a reliable driver.

On this cold grey morning, we were driving down a steep hill when we came up behind a convoy of three olive green jeeps. In front was a strange vehicle looking like an ancient Ford Popular convertible. It had Chinese characters written down the length of its long bonnet. The other two vehicles were poor Romanian copies of Land Rovers. All three vehicles were full of uniformed police and plain clothed *Sigurimi* armed with Kalashnikovs.

One of the first golden rules of driving in Albania that I learned was never to break a convoy. To do so, lay yours and the following vehicles open to isolation and ambush. Wherever the lead vehicle went, you followed nose to tail.

Don't overtake the Sigurimi Pierrino, I said to myself willing the front vehicle to hold back behind the police vehicles. As if to defy me, the Talbot overtook the convoy. *You bloody fool Pierrino!*

I had no option but to follow the Talbot. Not daring to look at the police, I stuck as close as I could to the little car. Miraculously all seemed well until we were about a mile down the road. Then, with a frenetic beeping of their horns, the police vehicles drove past us and blocked the road. Suddenly we were surrounded by angry men waving automatic weapons. I sat as still as death.

Through the Defender's windscreen, I could see poor Pierrino being manhandled and shouted at by the *Sigurimi*. He was clearly terrified. Unable to help him, I felt cowardly and useless. Then, when it seemed as if we were all about to be shot, the furious policemen jumped back into their vehicles and sped off in the direction of Bajram Curi. I never did find out what was said or done by whom to cause the secret police to stop so suddenly. Nevertheless, I thanked the Almighty for His intervention even though I am an agnostic.

"Do you think there was a chance we could have been shot?"

I asked Enzio, our Albanian interpreter.

"Oh yes," the serious young man replied. "It would have been reported that we tried to drive through a checkpoint.

One last event occurred to add to the bizarre nature of that eventful trip to Bajram Curi. On arrival in the town, we had to find a secure location to leave the Land Rover overnight. The only place where it would be safe from the thieves who infested this mountain region was the secret police compound. Once there, we were greeted by the same *Sigurimi* officers who had threatened us earlier on the mountain road. This time, though, they were all smiles and handshakes as if nothing untoward had ever happened.

Human beings are very adaptable and given time, we can adjust to almost any situation. This was the case when I was navigating Albania's treacherous roads. Weaving in and out of huge potholes and passing within inches of unfenced two-thousand-foot drops soon became second nature to me.

Whether it was from snarling farm dogs attacking the Land Rover's tyres, hostile children hurling stones or picking my way through a recent rockfall, it all became part of every day life. There was one exception to this rule however. I only had to do it a couple of times, but driving through one sad little town called Fushe Arrez (pronounced Fushte Ahvez) was always a frightening experience.

The main road passed right through the town with the main square about halfway down. The fall of communism caused the local state-run pulp mill to close. Being the only source of work, this had created wide-scale unemployment and deep bitterness. Driving slowly through the hostile crowds of unemployed men in the square, I could sense their barely suppressed anger that threatened to explode into violence against our convoy. One wrong move, or an accidental nudge of any of those men by a car bumper would have caused a violent riot to erupt.

Whilst travelling in the daytime had such scary moments, night driving was in a class of its own. This was a country where only the main centres of population like Tirane and Shkodra had any form of street lighting. Everywhere else was in total darkness at night. This made the roads very dangerous. None of them had any markings or warning signs. Round the next bend might be a horse drawn cart, a herd of cattle or cyclists weaving all over the road.

Easily the most dangerous vehicles on these nocturnal roads were the ancient communist built trunks. Their headlamps were either full on or off without the capitalist luxury of a dipping switch. When one of these vehicles approached, they would kill their lights completely and expect the other vehicle to do the same. Both vehicles would then attempt to avoid a collision using blind navigation. On numerous occasions, I would dip the Land Rover's lights only to be blinded by the approaching truck's headlights switched back on in an angry confrontation. One of the many mysteries of my time in the Balkans was how I avoided having a serious or fatal accident. However, I did make it back in one piece, after one more scare.

Just a few days before I was due to return to the UK, I returned to Bajram Curri. This was to deliver a consignment of basic medicines to the town's hospital. The first part of the journey was uneventful until the road entered a thickly wooded mountain area. Lulled into a false sense of security, I turned over the whole trip in my mind. Although tense and and often frightening at times, it certainly had not been at all bad. Nothing terrible, such as a serious injury or a robbery, had befallen me.

At that moment, we rounded a bend to be confronted by a tree lying across the road. Too neatly placed for it to be accidental, this was definitely an ambush.

"Back up, back up," said my passenger tensely. "They'll have this area pegged out for their marksmen."

He was an ex-military man who had seen service in Northern Ireland before joining the charity. That's what the IRA did in Ulster he explained later.

I reversed back, then waited, revving the engine while the serviceman and our Albanian interpreter jumped out and ran over to shift the tree. The time this took seemed like hours but was only a couple of minutes at the most. All the time, I expected to be hit by a volley of shots.

Fortunately, the tree was little more than a sapling which

was easily pulled off the road. No sooner had the two men jumped back in the Defender than I put my foot down hard on the accelerator. We must have been half a mile down the road before they managed to shut the vehicle's door.

I have often wondered why we had been spared. It was as if I had a guardian angel watching over me. However, I think there was a much more mundane reason:

The ambush must have been closed for lunch.

THE NABATEAN URN

Harry Darrowby or Harold St John Leadbetter Darrowby to give him his full title, had been a regular in *The Pheasant* pub for many years. Now in his early eighties, he could certainly be described as 'sprightly'. Always a very dapper man, given to wearing a tweed suit and waistcoat even on hot days, Harry had a distinctive fat laugh and a wicked sense of humour. Bumping into him once on his way home from the pub, John Fitzherbert, one of his old mates, asked him how he was.

"Not too good actually," Harry replied. "Had to have one of those camera thingies shoved up inside my tum." Then he added with his characteristic chuckle: "Good job it wasn't a box brownie."

That was Harry all over, he could be relied upon to make light of even the most serious situation. He was also an excellent raconteur, especially with a couple of glasses of his favourite whisky inside him. Unlike Fitzherbert, John stuck to Highland Park from Scotland's most northerly distillery in Orkney.

Every Saturday, a group of *The Pheasant's* regulars met at the pub for 'a few drinks and a natter' as Harry put it. Bertie Mullins was alive then and that old bullshitter, Cyril Peters who always liked to pretend he was something in the secret services. Oh yes, and there was that writer chappie Nick. Didn't always get much out of that one. Fond of listening though. On this particular Saturday, the group got on to the subject of archaeology and ancient artefacts.

"I can't think what the fascination is in all those pots and old things they dig up," Cyril Peters said.

"Well, that's because you don't see it through an archaeologist's eyes," Bertie replied. "When one of these archaeologists handles an ancient bowl, he doesn't just see some piece of clay or china but a whole civilisation stretching back thousands of years."

"You know, that reminds me of when Angela and I were

living in Quahrain," Harry Darrowby said.

"You mean that godforsaken bit of sand just next to the Empty Quarter?" Cyril asked.

"That's right, squeezed in between Yemen and Saudi," Harry said. "You wouldn't want those two for neighbours I can tell you. Quarrelsome buggers. The place has changed a lot now of course. This was just after the old sultan had been turfed out by his son in the early seventies. Good job too. The old boy hated progress and had closed down the only school for girls in the whole country shortly after we arrived. His eldest son, Mohammed Bin Badar was all for progress. So he and his SAS mates waited until the old boy went off on a shopping trip to London and toppled him.

"One of the first things, his son did as the new Sultan was to authorise a big archaeological dig just outside the capital. The site was a sort of lost city called Qmran, a bit like Petra sitting bang on the spice and frankincense routes. That's why the Nabateans built it there, to control the traffic. The old man forbade anyone to go near or touch the place when he was in charge. On pain of death and all that.

"So I think his son did it partly to spite him. No love lost there I can tell you! His dad had Mohammed banged up under house arrest way down in the south of the country for years. Mind you, the new Sultan was no Philistine. He wanted his people to see that part of their culture and country's history. That's why he had the place excavated. Something his dad would never have understood.

"He hired the top man from the British Museum, Sir Melvyn Tonabrand, to oversee the dig. He had his wife in tow, that was the part of the deal you see. She was that crime novelist, Maria Madrigal. Wrote a very good thriller based on the place if I remember rightly."

"*Death in The Dunes*," John Fitzherbert interjected.

"That's the one! I was down there working for one of the big Gulf trading houses. With the country opening up and modernising, there was a lot of business to be had putting together deals for all sorts of stuff they needed. Anyway, Angela, my wife, became very good friends with Maria. As a result, we spent quite a bit of time in each other's company.

"To tell you the truth, Melvyn was quite a bit older than Maria and found her rather demanding at times, if you get my drift. Especially in all that heat. There wasn't any air conditioning in those days. Well, Melvyn would often invite me back to his 'little lair' as he called it. Just a tent really, but it was where he could relax in my company. He took quite a shine to me. Fellow whisky drinker you see," Harry tapped the side of his nose confidentially.

He well remembered those convivial evenings in Melvyn's tent. The archaeologist had it set up at the actual Qmran dig. That was situated at the end of a long wadi filled with lush date plantations and surrounded by saw-toothed mountains.

"I think this excavation will be both my ultimate achievement and my swansong," Melvyn said holding his whisky glass up to the light.

"Why do you say that Melvyn, you've got years of digging left in you."

"I wish that were so Harry but my body and the doctors say otherwise. According to them, I'll be lucky to last until Christmas. Inoperable cancer."

"I'm sorry to hear that Melvyn," Harry said as indeed he was. During his time in Quahrain, he had developed a genuine affection for the archaeologist and a great respect for his wide knowledge of past civilisations. He also admired his ability to communicate that knowledge to Joe and Jane Public. In fact, Tonabrand's weekly series *Ancient Worlds Brought to Life* had become one of the unexpected hits of early British colour television.

"Come with me Harry, I've got something to show you," Melvyn said rising stiffly from his canvas chair. Harry followed him out of the tent to a large canvas marquee. Its entrance was guarded by two Quahrainis with breech-loading rifles. They were dressed in the traditional garb of tightly wrapped white turbans and flowing robes with curved khanja diggers strapped to their waists.

They stood down as the archaeologist greeted them entering the dim interior of the large tent. Harry knew this was where all the artefacts discovered during the dig were stored. Few were allowed inside this holy of holies of Sir Melvyn Tonabrand. He felt very privileged.

Neatly laid out across the sand floor were a large number of ancient pots, tools, utensils and weapons. "Quite a hoard," Melvyn said proudly. Harry nodded in agreement.

"The silent history of a long dead culture."

"I think it is what is known as a mute testimonial," Harry added.

"Yes, you could say that," Melvyn replied. "Although the Nabateans speak to me over the centuries when I handle any of these pieces. That's the beauty of being an archaeologist Harry, you converse directly with the past. Now, take your pick, and choose any one of these finds. Go on."

"You sure Melvyn?"

"Of course! Wouldn't say so otherwise. We'll soon be going our separate ways and I'd like you to have something to remember our friendship."

As Harry scanned the artefacts, an onion-shaped vase with a zig zag pattern caught his eye. He stepped forward and picked it up.

"Good choice," Melvyn said. "That's a fourth-century Nabatean burial urn."

The following year, the Darrowbies made one of their many moves across the Middle East. On that occasion, it was to another large trading company in the Iranian capital of Teheran. As always, the burial urn went with them. However, Angela insisted Harry kept it outside the house wherever they lived. There was something she disliked about it. She said it made her feel uncomfortable.

Harry put that down to the fact that she knew it was a burial urn. How he regretted telling her that! If only he had said it was some 'love vase' containing aphrodisiac, he was sure it would have then had pride of place on the mantlepiece.

It was while they were in Teheran that news came through of Sir Melvyn Tonabrand's death at the relatively early age of seventy.

"Poor Maria, I'll send her a condolence card," Angela said, then added, "I told you that urn was bad news Harry."

"His death had nothing to do with him giving me that urn," he protested. "It was cancer that killed him not bad karma."

"Call me illogical if you like, but I know the two are connected," Angela insisted. Try as he might, there was no shifting his wife from her belief.

Some years later they finally quit the Middle East to settle back in England. This move had been prompted mainly by the growing instability of the region but also because their family had been enlarged by the addition of a son and daughter.

Fortune had favoured Harry when he landed a job with Periam Ceramics as their Industrial and Marketing Development Director. This fast growing company was seeking to expand its industrial ceramics range into the Middle Eastern and Southern American markets.

"We'll spearhead this growth with an extensive all media marketing campaign," the CEO Saul Biedermann explained to Harry. "You know the Middle East and industrial marketing so I expect you to find the right type of agency for this campaign."

As it turned out, Harry found an advertising agency that seemed to foot the bill admirably. Flynn, Curlew, Robinson was a well established agency that had mounted many successful campaigns for a number of multinational conglomerates in publications such as Forbes, Time and The Wall Street Journal.

'My contact at the agency was a young chap who was one of their account executives called Roddy O'Toole," Harry explained then paused, holding up his empty whisky glass. "I'll have another

Highland Park if you don't mind Karen."

Twenty-one-year-old Roddy O'Flynn had neatly cut blond hair and an open face that invited you to trust him. Allied to this was a gentle, empathetic smile that would melt even the hardest of hearts.

Unlike most people, Roddy O'Toole had the ability to say exactly the right thing even at the most difficult of times. Whether it was the demise of a pet dog or even a parent, he could be relied upon to come up with exactly the right phrase to soothe a bereaved owner or relative. With such a kind demeanour and silver tongue, it was no wonder people trusted this 'natural gentleman'. That included Harry who took to Roddy in a big way.

"He was the sort of chap you would happily leave in charge of a couple of bars of gold bullion and know he wouldn't do a runner," Harry said to his circle of drinking companions. "But, as you may already have guessed, young Roddy was not all he seemed. In fact he was, to use a technical term, an absolute rotter. I didn't know that at the time of course."

Periam's offices were situated in a small science park at the edge of the Berkshire town of Abingdon. This suited Harry very well since he was living at Fallsworth, a Thameside village just fifteen minutes drive away. His modern office had large picture windows with views of the beautiful surrounding countryside. He decided this would be the ideal home for the Nabatean Urn he had just rediscovered.

"It looked rather sad gathering dust on a work bench in my garage. Since I knew that Angela would never have it in the house, I decided to give it pride of place in my office."

A day or so later, he and Roddy O'Toole had their first meeting in Periam's offices. It was to discuss the overall strategy for the company's Middle Eastern marketing campaign.

"I say, that's an interesting piece of pottery you've got there," Roddy exclaimed indicating the Nabatean urn sitting over by the window.

"Yes, that's a gift from on old friend," Harry said. "I keep it here to remind myself of him."

"Mind if I have a closer look?" Roddy asked. "Ancient pottery is a bit of a speciality of mine."

"No, go ahead," Harry said. "Just don't drop it."

Rising from his seat, O'Toole walked over and picked up the urn "Hm, a fine piece. Second century Nabatean if I'm not mistaken."

Harry was impressed. Except for being a couple of centuries out, that was exactly how Melvyn Tonabrand had described it.

"Might be worth quite a lot," Roddy said. "I could get it valued if you like."

"No, it's alright, I'd never sell it anyway," Harry replied.

"Be wise if only for insurance purposes," Roddy pressed.

There was something about the young man's eagerness to hold on to the urn that unsettled Harry.

"Look old chap, thanks for the advice, but let's stick to advertising, shall we? That's what you're here for after all."

"Yes of course," Roddy said backing off. "I tend to get a bit carried away when I see a beautiful old artefact like that. Still, if you change your mind, just call me."

"What do you think that urn is worth?" Harry asked O'Toole as he escorted him out of the building after their meeting.

"Probably nothing, forget it," he replied. "But on the odd occasion, they can fetch several thousands at auction." He had sounded offhand but Roddy knew he had successfully sown the seed of avarice in Harry's mind. Now all he needed was the patience to watch it grow.

"It's funny how fate plays a role in our lives," Harry said to the others. "About six months after that meeting I was presented with a whacking great bill from my daughter's private school. For *extracurricular activities.* More like extracurricular highway robbery if you ask me. Still it had to be paid. The problem was I did not have the readies on me there and then."

He told Angela about the encounter with O'Toole and what he had said about the urn.

"You might as well get him to value it," she said. "If he's right and it is worth thousands, it would solve the school fees problem wouldn't it?"

So, at her urging, he arranged with O'Toole to bring the urn to London and have it valued by O'Toole's uncle who was the C.E.O. of the agency.

"You see, my Uncle William is quite a specialist in these ancient artefacts," Roddy explained smoothly.

Harry Darrowby was generally a pretty shrewd man, so agreeing to an informal valuation might seem an inexplicable lapse of judgement. However, Roddy O'Toole came across as such a trustworthy individual. That he might be a conman did not enter Harry's brain.

"I should have smelt a rat from the very start," he said ruefully. "But to be honest, I really didn't think the urn was worth much. I remember I carried it all the way on the Paddington train in nothing more than a Spar carrier bag.

William Flynn was a tall man in his mid-sixties. The network of veins on his ruddy cheeks spoke of a lifelong acquaintance with spirits.

"The Middle Eastern campaign seems to be going very well," Flynn said.

"Yes, I think so," Harry agreed.

"Well, if it's all the same to you, we'll talk about that later. In the meantime I would love to have a look at that legendary urn of yours."

Placing his carrier bag on the boardroom table, Harry carefully removed the Nabatean urn.

"May I?" Flynn asked reverently taking hold of the ancient piece. "Hm, a lovely example of Nabatean pottery."

"It was a personal gift from my old friend Melvyn Tonabrand," Harry explained.

"The very best from the very best," Flynn said admiringly.

"I'm surprised he parted with it."

"We were very good mates."

"I should say you were," Flynn exclaimed. "I need to give its potential value some thought. Mind if I keep it for a few days?"

"I'd rather hang on to it if you don't mind," Harry said guardedly. "I can always bring it back at a later date."

"Of course!" Flynn said expansively. "Let's just leave it with my p.a. Siobhan until the end of the meeting. Just for safekeeping."

Harry missed the hard, calculating glint in Flynn's eyes as he said this pressing a buzzer on his desk. Moments later Siobhan, an attractive brunette in her thirties entered the room wheeling a well-stocked drinks trolley.

"A Highland Park for you Mr Darrowby?" she asked.

"With a splash of spring water if you don't mind."

After dispensing the drinks, she left carrying the urn.

This marked the start of a long afternoon of conversation about the Periam campaign interspersed with many whiskies in large cut glass tumblers. Or rather, that was Harry's hazy recollection of what passed at that meeting.

In fact, it was late the next morning when he finally came to in his own bed. Harry had no recollection of the return journey from London.

"Well, a fine state you were in last night!" His wife said angrily as she handed him a black coffee.

"Was I?" He asked timidly, not really wishing to hear the details.

"I assume you sold the damned thing," she said. "I hope you got a decent price."

"Sold what?" He had no idea what she was talking about.

"The urn of course! That's what you went up to London for wasn't it?"

"No, I went to get it valued. I didn't sell it."

"Then where is it, Harry?" Angela asked in exasperation.

"You certainly didn't bring it home with you."

"I don't rightly know," he said with a sick feeling creeping up from his stomach like silent death.

Gradually, the memory of his visit to London with the urn returned to haunt him. The train journey with the urn in the Spar carrier bag sitting beside him. That was followed by William Flynn's effusive greeting.

"Yes, they really had seen me coming," Harry said.

Then the most painful memory of all, the sight of the urn being removed from the office by the trusty Siobhan, for safekeeping. *For safekeeping! Ha!* Too bloody right! Safe from its rightful owner Harold St John Darrowby Esquire!. After that, just a drink soaked haze of one Highland Park after another. Bastards!

When he tried phoning William Flynn a little later, he got no further than Siobhan the p.a.

'I'm afraid Mr Flynn is currently unavailable," she said in her soft, honey sweet voice.

"Well that's okay Siobhan, all I need do is pick up my urn which you took away for safekeeping during my visit."

"I'm sorry, Mr Darrowby, I don't follow you," she said, her voice reflecting genuine bafflement. She was good this one, well worth whatever Flynn paid her.

"Come on Siobhan, surely you remember taking the urn away after you brought in the drinks. Flynn said it was for safekeeping remember?"

"Well, I certainly remember bringing in the drinks. As for removing an urn, I have absolutely no recollection of that."

"I have to say, I find that very strange," Harry said grinding his teeth in frustration. "No matter, perhaps I can speak to Roddy O'Toole."

I'm afraid that won't be possible either," Siobhan said apologetically.

"Why not for goodness sake? Don't tell me he's been swallowed up by a black hole!"

"No Mr Darrowby, I thought you knew that Mr O'Toole left

the agency last month."

"But he was at that meeting the day before yesterday. He was the one who arranged it and the valuation by William Flynn."

"I think you must be mistaken Mr Darrowby, there's no record of him being at that meeting and I certainly don't recall him being there. Do you have any paperwork for this urn?"

"If you say I didn't hand it over why would there be any paperwork?" Harry asked.

The ensuing silence told Harry that Siobhan knew she had been been caught out. It also told him he was being blanked.

"I'll tell Mr Flynn that you phoned," she said after an awkward silence. "I'm sure he'll get back to you at the earliest opportunity."

"I never managed to speak to either Flynn or O'Toole ever again," Harry said to his little audience in the pub. "The agency assigned me some bland dimwit called Hawkins as my replacement account manager after that."

"It was obviously a stitch-up, so why didn't you speak to your boss?" Nick asked. "As an important client, surely he could have leant on the agency to return the urn."

"Well, that would have been a bit embarrassing if you think about it," Harry said. "He could well have looked askance at me for doing a bit of antique dealing in the firm's time. In fact, it would probably have cost me my job."

"You didn't think of going to the police then?"

"Angela was all for me doing that, but as I told her at the time, there was a big problem there. You see, I brought the urn into Blighty as a personal effect without any accompanying paperwork. If I had reported its theft to the police, customs and excise would have been on my back quicker than you could say con man!"

"In other words you were well and truly stuffed," Cyril Peters said.

"Like the proverbial Christmas turkey," Harry chuckled. He took a long, thoughtful sip of his whisky.

"As for Messrs O'Toole and Flynn, they had disappeared with my urn like the snows of spring."

A few months after that fateful meeting, Harry had the galling experience of seeing his Nabatean urn in all its untouchable glory. Flicking through a glossy country magazine, he came across a feature on ancient Middle Eastern artefacts. It was sponsored by Somersby & Co., a notable and well respected London auction house who had recently mounted a sale of such items.

Occupying half a page of the feature was a picture of Harry's stolen urn. It was still clearly recognisable despite being expertly cleaned up. As if to mock him, the accompanying description said:

Second Century Nabatean Burial Urn formerly owned by The Estate the late William Flynn of Hederley, Buckinghamshire. Sold to a private buyer for £70,000.

Seventy thousand quid! Harry thought his heart was going to stop. The Somersby's representative he spoke to gave little away, citing client confidentiality. He had better luck in tracking down what happened to William Flynn. Apparently, his body had been discovered in the bedroom of a Surrey hotel with that of a certain Mrs Siobhan Jackson. It seemed that both parties had died of barbiturate poisoning. Their untimely deaths had happened just two months after that meeting with Harry.

As for the Nabatean Urn, that did not stay in its new owner's hands for long either. Within a few months, Somersby and Co's Los Angeles office had it up for auction. This time it was by orders of the executors of the estate of the Late Cyrus Valentino a former dot com millionaire and health fanatic. He had been found dead on his exercise bike from a heart attack just two days after his thirtieth birthday.

The next owner was a small Swedish museum of antiquities. It suffered a catastrophic fire five months after purchasing the urn. It was then forced to sell the piece to raise funds for the necessary rebuilding after the fire.

Over the next two years, the Nabatean urn passed through the hands of four more owners, all of whom suffered major misfortunes within six months of taking ownership of the artefact.

Finally, it was acquired by the Quahraini Government for its newly established Qmran Museum. It has resided there ever since without causing any further mishap.

"Presumably, now the urn is back home, it's at peace," Harry concluded. "You see, nobody associated with it survived or prospered for very long, particularly the ones who nicked it."

"Except for Roddy O'Toole. You didn't say what happened to him," Nick said.

"He didn't escape either, I'm pleased to say," Harry replied. "At the same time the Quahrainis got the urn back, he was found in his flat very dead and very full of cocaine. So perhaps my loss was a blessing in disguise. Now I think it's my round." Harry reached into his pocket. "Ah, take a rain check on that, I seem to have left my wallet at home."

Nobody was in the least bit surprised at that revelation since it happened every week. Still, Harry Darrowby's stories were always worth a missed round. The tale of The Nabatean Urn was no exception to this rule.

THE THIRTEENTH APOSTLE
A Biblical Detective Story

Death and the afterlife was not how he imagined it. One moment D.S. Thomas Bethany was staring at the flash coming from the drug dealer's gun and the next he was walking down the wide corridor in a Jacobean mansion. The whole place smelled of fresh polish and echoed to the voices of officialdom.

He may not know what he was doing here, but what he did know was that his head ached like hell. *I suppose that's the consequence of having your brains splattered all over a crack house wall* he said to himself.

As he walked past a series of oak doors, he paused at one, quite why he simply did not know. It was a purely random choice, or so he thought. On it was a black plaque with the name *Inspector Peter Keys* in white writing. Without realising it, Bethany knocked on the heavy oak door.

"Come!" a voice shouted from inside the room.
Bethany opened the door and walked in. Sitting behind a large office desk was a man with white hair and quite startling blue eyes. He also had a neatly trimmed beard. Bethany put his age at about 65. Bit old even for a detective inspector, shouldn't he be retired by now? The name plaque on the desk simply said Peter Keys.

"I'm D.S. Thomas Bethany, sir."

"Yes, late of the Islington Drugs Squad, we know," Keys said impatiently. "That's why you're here, because you're brown bread son. But you knew that already didn't you?"

"So this is heaven?" Bethany asked.

Peter Keys had to laugh at that one, he really did.

"And what makes you think that's where you'd end up with your bloody awful record?"

"Is it hell then?"

"I do wish you could get away from these clichés, Thomas," Keys said with a heavy, universe-weary sigh. "All that simplistic stuff was dreamed up aeons ago by old men with long beards, big imaginations and even bigger egos. No, this is a sort of holding station before we decide where to send you next."

"So I'm in purgatory?" Thomas asked.

"Oh yes, if you must," Keys said irritably. "Anyway, I didn't call you in here to get into a big theological discussion. You have work to do my boy."

"How can I work if I'm dead?" Thomas asked.

"Oh so you think that getting murdered lets you off the hook does it?" Keys asked in mock amazement. "No that's just the start of it D.S. Bethany. Now we have a juicy little two-thousand-year-old cold case for you to solve."

"But I don't do cold cases! I'm on the drugs squad," Bethany protested.

"Correction you *were* on the drugs squad until Black Harry blew your brains out for double-crossing him," Keys said quietly. "Now you're going to do a cold case for us."

"Supposing I refuse?" Thomas asked.

"Do you really want to see what Hell's like?" Keys asked with a wicked smile.

Suddenly, Bethany found himself in a terrifyingly dark and cold place where naked, blood-smeared demons were disembowelling men and women alive. Then one of the demons with a machete turned and advanced on him. He could not take his eyes off the belt around his midriff. It had freshly cut genitalia dangling from it.

"No, no," Thomas said quickly feeling quite faint.

"I thought not," Keys replied genially. "So, let's get down to the case in hand, shall we? Now it concerns a bloke called Jesus Nazareth…."

"What Jesus Christ?" Thomas asked incredulously.

"Yes that's right, Jesus of Nazareth, Son of God saviour of the Universe yadda, yadda, yadda."

Thomas Bethany had not been a practising Christian since he was a child and did not even believe in life after death. Nevertheless, he was shocked at Peter Keys' approach to Christ and Christianity. Wouldn't he be struck down by God or something?

"No is the answer," Keys said. "I won't be struck down by

divine lightning. Don't worry, Thomas, I know exactly what's going on in your head or what's left of it. Oh by the way, that headache is the aftermath of being shot by a high-velocity bullet, it'll soon pass. Now, you obviously know the basics of Jesus' story. How a local lad from humble beginnings as a provincial carpenter makes good and becomes The Messiah and then gets offed by the occupying forces with the connivance of the local religious mafia."

"Well, I wouldn't quite put it like that…."

"No of course you wouldn't, nor would we really because we don't believe life is quite as simple as that. Which is why we want you to go down there to Palestine and find out exactly what happened and who's holding the smoking gun, so to speak."

"But don't you know already?" Thomas asked. "Aren't you all seeing and all that."

"Doesn't work like that here, I'm afraid," Keys said ruefully. " The Afterlife, as you would call it, is a very complicated place with many competing departments, none of whom know what the other had for breakfast. How did the Bible put it? *'In my Father's House, there are many mansions.'* So, D. S. Bethany, all you have to do is find out who did what in the Jesus case, and you'll be well on the way to redeeming yourself for being a bent, conniving copper and philanderer."

"But how do I get around and buy things down there? I won't have any money."

"Use your mind," Keys replied. "Just shut your eyes and imagine there are some shekels in your hand and there will be. Want to get into Caiphas' house? Just shut your eyes and imagine it and sure enough you'll be there. Now if there's nothing else…."

"Just one question sir."

"Yes, what is it?"

"Well, why do you want to know what really happened to Jesus?"

"The truth Thomas, that's all. The Eternal Verity."

Without a break, Thomas Bethany found himself standing in a dusty street lined on either side with sandy-coloured mud houses. A mercilessly hot sun was beating down on him and glaring off the road. He was really grateful for the coarse, loose-fitting robe and sandals that he found he was now wearing.

"So this is Palestine," he said to himself and scratched his face thoughtfully. To his surprise discovered he now had a full black beard. As he stood there, taking in his surroundings, he saw a group of what he took to be Roman Legionnaires marching towards him in a cloud of dust. Leading them was a burly coarse featured man who was their triplicarius as sergeants were known in the Roman Army.

The sergeant came up close to Thomas and spoke directly into his face giving him the full benefit of his garlicky halitosis.

"What's the matter sonny, never seen a crucifixion detail before? Why don't you tag along and watch the fun eh?"

"Who's being crucified? Jesus of Nazareth?"

"What's that you said?" The triplicarius asked

"I just asked if you were crucifying Jesus that's all."

"You being funny friend? Why would we crucify someone who we nailed up last year? Here, Tinctus, I think we've got one of those Jewish stirrers from that weirdo Jesus sect. Tie him up, and he can keep this other scrote company at Golgotha."

Before he knew it, Thomas was being grasped by two of the legionnaires and bound with ropes. He had to do something very quickly. He closed his eyes and imagined he was in the centre of Jerusalem.

Suddenly, the soldiers found themselves wrestling with an empty length of rope. Their captive had completely vanished.

"You dozy bastards!" screamed the triplicarius. "You can't even keep hold of your own dicks! Get on after him."

"But where sir? He just disappeared."

"That's all we bloody need," the triplicarius muttered, wiping the sweat from his dust-streaked face. Ever since they had nailed up that troublemaker from Nazareth, there had been persistent rumours that Jesus was not actually dead. That somehow, his family and followers had brought him back to life and spirited him away. Now, he had his very own little would-be Messiah doing a vanishing act, and that was before they even had the pleasure of crucifying him.

"The centurio's going to love this!"

The first thing that Thomas was aware of was the overpowering stench. It was a mixture of cooking meat, human ordure and camel dung. He was in a narrow alleyway, flanked on both sides by wine shops, butchers and food stalls. It was very crowded and he found himself being jostled this way and that. Then he felt the hand grasping at his belt and the purse that was hanging from it. He grabbed the hand and pulled. It belonged to a scrawny arm of an emaciated man in his twenties. The thief's mean bearded face registered startled surprise as he tried to escape.

The pickpocket lunged at Thomas with a wicked looking dagger in his other hand. The detective was too quick for him. Grabbing the other arm, he banged the thief roughly against a nearby wall scattering some clay pots causing the nearby stall holder to shout angrily.

"Want to try your luck do you sonny?" Thomas snarled through gritted teeth. Then in one deft movement snapped the man's wrist. The thief dropped his weapon with an agonised scream. Thomas released his arms and, letting the man fall, kneed him in the groin on the way down for good measure.

Picking the knife up, Thomas began to walk up the street. He noticed that he was no longer jostled and the crowds parted before him. A mixture of awe and fear now showed on people's faces when he looked at them.

"Nice work friend," an oily voice said in his ear. He turned to see a rotund man in his thirties dressed in what were obviously fine robes. That and his carefully trimmed beard showed this person to be of some standing.

"I could do with someone like you to guard me and my business," the man said. "Interested?"

"Depends who you are doesn't it," Thomas replied.

"Judas Iscariot, I'm an important trader in the city."

"But you're d...." Thomas started to blurt out and then checked himself.

"I'm what?" Iscariot asked his tone sharpening.

"I just meant to say that, for such an obviously important man you're in quite a rough area of town."

"Needs must," Iscariot replied enigmatically. "Come, allow me to show you the hospitality of my house. It's not far from here. By what name are you called?"

"Carausus of Attrebatum," Thomas replied without hesitation whilst secretly wondering where that little lie came from.

Judas' house was an oasis of coolness and peace in the bustling heart of Jerusalem. It had a simple and almost run-down exterior, but when they passed through the main gate, the interior opened out into a large courtyard with many green plants and a fountain quietly chuckling in the centre. An aged retainer led them through to a domus. This was a relaxation room in the Roman style with reclining couches.

Without bidding, food was brought in by a pretty girl with dark oval eyes and partially covered black ringlets of hair. As she knelt to place food in front of Thomas, he caught the faint smell of an exotic but unidentified perfume.

"That is Ruth," Iscariot said. "I see she pleases you."

"It is a strange man who is not pleased by a pretty woman," Thomas replied.

"Yes and there are many such strange men amongst the Syrians and the Greeks," Judas said with a chuckle. "So Carausus you speak Hebrew with a foreign tongue do you not?"

"Attrebatum is far from here on that misty island the Romans call their Province of Britannia."

"So what brings you to Jerusalem?"

"I became tired of the cold and the wet, so travelled here with the Phoenician traders hoping to find work in Jerusalem and also my family."

"How so if you are not of this land?"

"Originally, I came from here before being sold into slavery as a child. My home is actually Nazareth."

Judas paused momentarily before putting a grape in his mouth and looked sharply at Thomas and then spoke slowly and quietly: "It's not wise to admit such a thing Carausus."

"Why?"

"You ask that question in the light of recent events? You must have been very far from here."

"Then please enlighten me," Thomas said.

"A dangerous revolutionary movement had to be finally crushed last year. It was led by a Nazarene called Jesus or Yeshu as some people say. Although he came from humble beginnings, he was both clever and cunning. He had to be stopped."

"Stopped?"

"Yes, stopped," Judas said with finality. "And stop him we did. The Romans finished the job by crucifying him last year. So, unless you wish to suffer a similar fate, I suggest you forget all about being from Nazareth and just tell people you are from Britannia."

There was a long silence whilst both men ate the bread, cheese and dried fish in front of them. Thomas was glad of this so that he could take mental stock of the situation. He had only been on the case five minutes, and already, the traditional story of Jesus' death was unravelling.

Far from hanging himself in shame, Judas had obviously gone on to bigger and better things. *He's really put those thirty pieces of silver to good use,* Thomas thought grimly. Still, he had to admit it seemed a more plausible outcome. Who was this *we* that Judas said had stopped Jesus' "revolution"? Thomas wondered.

There was also something else bothering him. Wasn't it a little fortuitous that he just happened to bump into Judas like that? Almost as if the whole thing was planned. Also, it was as if he was speaking the words and performing the actions of a complete stranger. Where had all that back story about him living in Roman Britain come from? History had been his worse subject at school and he had absolutely no knowledge of the Romans or anybody else. Yet here he was spouting on about living in "misty Britannia" and travelling with the Phoenicians as if he had lived there yesterday.

"Judging by your little performance in the street, violence is one of your main skills."

"I know how to handle myself with thieves and murderers," Thomas replied. "I was one of the enforcing guards of our great chief Verica."

Judas studied Thomas with narrowed eyes. He was sure Carausus was not just some thuggish palace guard but a man of intelligence and animal cunning.

"Well Carausus, I have an interesting little task for you," Judas said delicately peeling a grape. "And if you are successful, as I am sure you will be, many rewards will follow."

"What is this task you speak about?" Thomas asked.

"You're a clever man and I think you can guess that," Judas said teasingly.

"Rooting out Jesus' remaining followers?"

"Quite correct, I knew you were a clever man," Judas replied. "I said we had stopped this Nazarene's revolution, but there is always fire under the ashes ready to flare up given the slightest opportunity. There are still plenty of his followers scattered around not just in Judea and Samaria, but as far as Damascus and Athens. Who knows, the contagion may even have spread to your misty isle of Britannia. We want you to find and kill them."

"We?" Thomas asked hesitantly. It was not wise to appear too intelligent or else he might just be the next candidate for crucifixion.

"Jesus was a very clever man who said and did many wise things before his death. But, contrary to what his followers believed he was not always right," Judas said warming to his theme. "And one example was his statement that no man could serve two masters. After all, I am a case in point. On the one hand, I serve the Sanhedrin and the High priests and on the other, the Romans.

"Like your great chief Verica, they both need enforcers who possess both cunning and resources. So, what do you say Carausus? Will you accept this task?"

"I will do as you say," Thomas replied.

"Mind that you do," Judas said with an edge to his voice. "Or it will go very hard with you."

We'll see about that, thought Thomas.

Later on, he was shown to his room off the main courtyard by Ruth. As he followed the girl, he admired the lithe way she walked. His room was quite spacious and lit by oil lamps. The barred window looked out on lush vegetation. The bed was hard and simple covered by colourful thin rugs.

"Your room master," Ruth said averting her eyes. "I am nearby to attend your every need. Just call me softly and I will come." At that, her almond eyes flickered upwards to hold him in a brief but unnerving stare. Then she was gone.

As it happened, Thomas did not have to call Ruth because she came to him later that night. This was a happy turn of events, he reflected as she flitted into his room and knelt by his bed.

"Carausus!" she whispered urgently. "Wake up!"

"I am awake," he replied and stretched his hand to caress her face but she caught his wrist before he could touch her.

"Meet me in the main market by the temple steps at noon tomorrow and I will take you to Yeshu's followers. Christ, be with you, friend."

Then, frustratingly, she vanished yet again.

The next morning after breakfast, Judas summoned Thomas into his office, a large room leading off from the main courtyard. It was light and airy, with shelves of scrolls lining the walls. A youth of about twenty with girlish looks and dark curly hair was waiting for them.

"This is Agapitos," Judas said by way of introduction. "He'll accompany you to make sure you come to no harm. He is one of those Greeks we were talking about yesterday so watch your back Carausus."

Agapitos giggled at this as he looked Thomas up and down suggestively. He could not imagine this effeminate young man protecting him from a neutered cat let alone a band of brigands. Of course Thomas knew that was not his real purpose which was to report back everything he did to Judas.

"Thirty pieces of silver," Judas said tossing a bag of money to Thomas. "That's what I started with and it should do you equally well."

"Where do I start?" Thomas asked.

"If I knew that, I wouldn't waste my money hiring you now would I?" Judas answered.

"I will assist the noble Carausus in every way I can," Agapitos said.

"Yes I'll wager you will," Judas replied. "In and out of bed."

Agapitos gave another lascivious giggle. Thomas found this was already getting on his nerves.

"May I suggest we travel to the Temple area my Lord Carausus," Agapitos said obsequiously.

"Very well," Thomas replied. "By the way what does your name mean?"

"In my native tongue it means Beloved, my Lord. And should you wish I can be your beloved."

Thomas stopped and turned to face the Greek full on: "Is that so?"

"Oh yes my Lord Carausus I would make you so happy as I have done with many other masters"

"Now hear me well Agapitos," Thomas said bringing out a knife from under his robes and holding it close to the Greek's face. "I am not your beloved and never will be. I don't lie with men and if you so much as touch me accidentally, I will slit you from your belly to your miserable little neck. Understood?"

Agapitos nodded and gulped. Rivulets of sweat trickled down his face.

"Good, let's go and find some of the Nazarene's followers. I don't think they'll be clustering around the Temple, so any idea where else to start?"

"We could try the village of Magdala, that's where Jesus' widow Mary came from."

"His widow?" Thomas asked in shock.

"Oh yes my Lord, it is said she followed him everywhere. They were inseparable."

Thomas was astounded. The more he delved, the more the whole Jesus story was being shaken up like coloured glass in a kaleidoscope. Now he had to lose Agapitos before he met Ruth at the Temple. They had already changed direction away from the central area of the city. As Agapitos darted round the corner of a narrow street, Thomas shut his eyes and thought his way to the main Temple steps.

The next moment he was standing there in the shade of a column. He drew the hood of his cloak over his head. It was insufferably hot and the smells of slaughtered animals, burning flesh and human waste filled his nostrils in a nauseous brew. He had no idea what the time was, but hoped that it was not too long before Ruth arrived.

"Looking for a good time mister?" It was the ageless street pitch of every whore and streetwalker since time immemorial. This time the voice was familiar. Thomas turned to see Ruth, also with her head covered smiling at him.

"Only ten shekels mister and I'll make all your troubles melt away. Come on now before those naughty Greeks find you."

Tugging at his robe, she hurried away into the maze of narrow, thronged streets running off from the main Temple square. Just past a fishmonger's stall she turned into a doorway. Thomas followed her running up a flight of stairs and through another door. After climbing a further flight of stairs and they were out in a roof garden shaded from the sun by a canopy covered in vines.

"Slow down Ruth, what's this all about?" Thomas said.

"My real name is not Ruth, that is just for that swine Judas' household. I am Esther a cousin of Mary Magdalene and I am a new follower of Jesus the Nazarene. Now we must hurry to see the others."

"But why are you doing this? You know that Judas has ordered me to seek out and kill all his followers."

" I know you are no more capable of obeying that evil man than your name is Carausus."

"How do you know?"

"My heart tells me," she said emphatically hitting her chest with the palm of her hand. "My heart tells me that you are a good man who will not harm us."

"You cannot possibly know that!" Thomas replied. However, Ruth or Esther was no longer listening. She had turned and was hurrying through another door that took them onto the roof of an adjoining house. Thomas lost track of the doors and steps through which they passed. Then suddenly, they were in a dimly lit second floor room. There was little furniture and several men rose as they entered.

"Who is this Esther?" asked a large bearded man with muscular biceps. "You know it is not safe to bring strangers here."

"This is the man Carausus I told you about Peter, he wishes to join us," Esther replied evenly.

"But he is from the traitor Judas' house! How can we trust him?" Peter exclaimed angrily.

"I am also from that house and you trust me," Esther retorted.

"That is true Peter," said one of the others, a dark wiry man.

"Thank you, Andrew," Esther replied.

"Let Carausus speak for himself," a handsome woman in her late thirties added.

"Very well Mary," Peter said. "So Carausus who are you and from where do you come?"

"I have returned from the Isle of Britannia to revisit my place of birth in Nazareth and try to find my family."

The disciples exchanged glances and Andrew asked: "So, if you are not a gentile then what is your Hebrew name?"

"I have long forgotten it having been sold into slavery as a very young child."

"And what is your business in Judas' house?" Peter asked.

"I accepted his offer of hospitality to be tricked into his service. He wishes me to seek out and kill all followers of Jesus the Nazarene."

"Well what are you waiting for friend?" Peter said presenting his body with his arms spread wide.

"I have no intention of carrying out his orders, merely to escape Judas' clutches. He sent his Greek spy Agapitos to accompany me and ensure I did what I was told but I gave him the slip."

Esther nodded at this.

"Whatever else, you must not return to Judas," Mary said to him. "And it is not safe to remain here for any of us. It will not take long for Agapitos or Iscariot's many other spies to seek us out."

"Yes, we must travel to see the Master, he will know what to do with this new disciple of ours," Peter said with a hint of irony. "We will leave after sunset."

"Where are we going?" Thomas asked.

"It is best you don't know that for now," Peter replied.

They left Jerusalem by one of the smaller city gates. Without doubt Judas would have put out the alert to watch for Carausus. The city guards would have been watching out for him with or without Agapitos. This gate was also guarded, but the soldiers were tired and seemed to have little interest in their task. Mary and Esther bribed them with some full wineskins and they waved the party and their donkeys through.

After travelling for several hours into the harsh, rock strewn landscape, Peter deemed it safe to call for a short halt. He seemed to have relaxed and appeared more amenable.

"So, now you know about me Peter, tell me about our little party," Thomas ventured.

He looked at Thomas for a long time before answering him as if weighing up whether he really could trust this stranger in their midst.

"I am the one our master calls The Fisherman for that was my trade," he said eventually. "The short man there is Andrew my brother he was also crew on my boat. And the woman is Mary of Magdala one of the master's closest followers."

"And where are we going?"

"To Har Nevo, the last resting place of The Prophet Moses. There we shall meet Jesus."

The journey through that unremittingly harsh landscape took a further two days before they reached the fertile Jordan Valley. On two occasions they had to hide in shallow valleys from Roman patrols.

Crossing the freezing waters of the River Jordan they then climbed for a further day until they reached the crest of a high mountain ridge.

"This is Har Nevo," Peter said to Thomas. The whole of Palestine was spread out beneath them in a truly breathtaking panorama. Riding along the ridge, they came to a simple stone building. In its single doorway stood a man that Thomas judged to be about five foot six.

Flinging herself from her donkey Mary Magdalene ran over to the man and fell at his feet wrapping her arms about his legs.

"Oh my Lord Jesus," she wept. Gently the man lifted Mary to her feet.

So this is Jesus, Thomas thought to himself. The man did not seem that impressive considering he was supposedly the Son of God. But then, what did Thomas expect? A tall, milky-skinned Aryan as depicted in countless stained glass windows. The truth was, he really had no clear idea. Then, as he came closer, he saw Jesus' eyes. In contrast to his dark olive complexion, they were light brown with flecks and held him with a riveting stare.

"Greetings Peter," Jesus said. "Greetings to you all."

Thomas then realised that another pillar of the traditional Biblical account of Jesus' death had collapsed. It was over a year since he had been crucified and was supposedly in heaven, yet here he was still on earth apparently living in a shepherd's hovel on top of a mountain.

"You have a new follower I see," Jesus said to Peter indicating Thomas.

"This is Carausus of Britannia," Peter said by way of introduction.

"You are welcome Carausus. Come closer so that I can embrace you properly."

Hesitantly, Thomas dismounted and walked over to Jesus who embraced him with both arms. Then, holding him at arms length Jesus looked into his face with those searching brown eyes. Thomas felt distinctly uncomfortable.

"So you are from that cold damp place the Romans call

Britannia," Jesus said.

"You know it?" Thomas asked in surprise.

"In my youth, I travelled there with my uncle Joseph to whom I was particularly close," Jesus replied. "Now you must be hungry, let us eat."

During the meal of fish, goat's cheese, olives and unleavened bread Thomas sat next to Jesus.

"I sense Carausus that you are not all you seem, that you are searching for something."

"The truth my Lord that is all," Thomas replied carefully.

"In this life, there are many different truths my friend," Jesus replied. "What is yours."

Somehow, Jesus' whole manner and those strange searching eyes made it impossible for Thomas to lie.

"I have been sent from another time by er… a higher authority to discover what became of you. Whether you were really crucified."

Jesus held his palms up to Thomas. The terrible wounds of the crucifixion nails still showed clearly.

"Is this not truth enough?" he asked.

Suddenly, Thomas felt very ashamed and very frightened. He had no business to be here and yet he was trapped by forces that were way beyond his control.

So Jesus *had* died on the cross then returned to life.

"The answer to your thoughts is yes Carausus, I did die and return to life but not in the way you might think. We have good healers who can keep a man in a deathlike state for days then bring him back to full health."

"You mean The Resurrection was a trick?" Thomas asked.

"Not a trick Carausus, just not how people will come to believe it to be."

"Are you not the Son of God then?"

"Of course I am," Jesus replied smiling gently. "Just as Peter, Andrew and all the others, even you, are His sons and Mary his Daughter. Now I must go and do my Father's work. I have many days travel to the east where I will be known by other names." Jesus said as he rose to his feet.

He picked up a leather bag and, placing food and a wineskin in it, slung the bag over his shoulder. The other disciples followed him outside the crude stone building. He embraced all the men for a final time before coming to Mary Magdala who fell at his feet again and wept. He lifted her up but she still clung to Jesus not wishing to let him go.

"Take me with you Jesus!"

"You know I can't Mary," he replied sadly. Releasing her, he turned to the east and began walking down the mountain slope.

Suddenly, a thick mist blew in obliterating the landscape. Within seconds, it was gone and so was The Messiah.

Peter Keys was not having a good time at all. The Director had been down to tear a strip off him. At six foot three with a truly menacing stare, The Director was a terrifying figure at the best of times. There was a rumour that he had not smiled for at least two millennia. Well, he certainly was not smiling now.

"I thought I told you Keys the last time this happened, with that nonsense over The Flood not to meddle and rewrite history. Now you have created an almighty mess with this Jesus story. Don't you realise that by sending in the policeman, you have created an anachronism, a thirteenth disciple! How's that going to run in the King James Bible?"

Wisely, Peter Keys did not answer the Director's rhetorical question. In fact, it was best not to say anything at all when the Director was in mid rant.

"Right, unless this sorry business is stopped now, the whole careful balance of history will be upset. So, unless you want to spend a quiet thousand years in the Heironymous Bosch Centre I suggest you get down there and sort it out personally and quickly."

Keys did not need to be told twice, and in the blink of an eye, he was in Palestine.

"Our work is finished here," Peter announced and the group began to move in a northerly direction. Thomas held back closing his eyes and within an instant, he was on the road just outside Jerusalem. His job was finished too and it was time to report to

Keys. How this would be done precisely he had no idea. Suddenly he was grabbed roughly by the shoulders.

"Got yer, yer little Jewish bleeder," a voice shouted in triumph. It was the Roman triplicarius with bad breath who had first arrested him. Desperately, Thomas tried to will himself elsewhere but it was no longer working. He struggled to free himself, but the Roman soldiers bound him tightly with coarse ropes.

"We'll take you to the Centurio, I'm sure you'll have a lot to say to him you Jewish scum!"

As he was half dragged through the streets of the city, Thomas lost his sandals and in no time his feet were painful and bleeding. Passing the various stalls the merchants jeered and spat at him. One threw a rotten orange that exploded against the side of his face. Clearly, they thought the Romans had caught a thief.

Finally, they arrived at a building Thomas knew only too well. It was Judas' house. Now there were two legionnaires guarding the half open door.

"Centurio there is he?" the triplicarius asked, and one of the guards nodded.

Thomas was dragged through the door. The scene in the courtyard was total chaos with smashed pottery jars and torn scrolls littering the paving slabs. The body of Agrapitos was draped over the side of the fountain lying face down in the water. The haft of a spear protruded from his rectum and the water was blood red.

Two soldiers pulled a familiar figure from one of the rooms. It was Judas, but he was no longer the cunning and ruthless spy master that had employed Thomas. This Judas was beaten and broken, his swollen face a mass of bruises. Behind this little group stood a Roman officer in all his finery. Staring into his eyes, Thomas realised that he knew this man only too well, for it was Peter Keys.

"Here he is Centurio," the triplicarius said triumphantly. "That little Jew who gave us the slip. He won't get away again."

"See that he doesn't if you know what's good for you."

Judas squinted up at Thomas through swollen eyes.

"So it was you who betrayed me!" he snarled, broken teeth

giving him a lisp. "You bastard."

"What should we do with him Sir. Crucify him?" one of the guards holding Judas asked.

"No, hang him from up there," Keys replied indicating a beam that protruded from the wall on the upper floor of the villa. Then, nodding towards Thomas he said: "In the meantime, I'd like to interrogate this man."

Keys walked into one of the rooms opening onto the courtyard and the guards dragged Thomas after him.

"Alright you can leave him with me," Keys said to the guards who reluctantly exited closing the door behind them.

Keys turned and looked at Thomas. He had to admit all that Roman clobber certainly suited him.

"Well Bethany, you really are a good detective aren't you?"

"Was," Thomas replied tersely. "What now?"

Keys did not answer immediately. The sounds of Judas choking to death accompanied by the shouts and laughter of the soldiers wafted through the open window.

"The operation has had to be closed down I'm afraid," Keys replied. "Such a waste after all your good work but there we are, orders are orders."

Just then the horrible noise of Judas' strangulation reached a crescendo and then stopped abruptly. A jovial cheer went up from the soldiers. Keys went to the door and opening it shouted to his subaltern:

"Triplicarius take this man away and crucify him!"

"You can't do that!" Thomas cried in horror.

"Sorry Thomas," Keys shrugged. "Needs must. It won't hurt much, promise."

As the soldiers marched him out through the courtyard, Thomas tried not to look at Judas dangling there with his swollen tongue hanging out of his bloodied mouth.

In the event, his crucifixion took a long time and he suffered a great deal of pain. Then, mercifully darkness swept over him.

Everyone from the surgeon down agreed it was a miracle that DC Bethany pulled through. Fortunately, Black Harry, the drug dealer had moved the gun slightly as he pulled the trigger causing the bullet to burrow through the right side of the detective's skull without mashing up the vital parts of his brain. What was even more of a miracle was that he emerged from his coma twelve days after the operation with all his faculties intact.

"Whose a lucky boy then?" his wife Carmen asked sitting on the side of his bed during her first visit. Funny, Thomas had forgotten quite how good looking she was. Not dissimilar to an older version of Ruth really. Suddenly, the whole Jesus episode came vividly rushing back from his first meeting with Judas to that dreadful crucifixion.

"They said you were as good as dead." Good old Carmen, never one to beat about the bush. "Do you remember anything, hun?"

"No," Thomas lied.

"Ah so all that stuff about angels is all a load of crap then."

"Yep," Thomas said.

"I'm popping down to the hospital shop, can I get you anything?"

"Yeah, a copy of the Sun," he said. "And a bar of Cadburys."

"The newspaper yes but sorry no can do with the chocolate. Nil by mouth."

In fact she did not even manage the Sun but brought a copy of The Telegraph instead.

"Oh what's this," he asked in irritation.

"That's all they had left. Anyway some good hard news instead of all those tits and scandal will do you good for a change. Got to go now hun. I'll be back tomorrow."

She kissed his bandaged forehead lightly and was gone.

Well that didn't take long, wonder who she's seeing? he thought as he opened the paper. Didn't know why he bothered, it was all the same stories: car bombs, lying politicians, celebrities buying African kids as trophy sons and daughters...

Then a news item halfway down the second page caught his eye:

"Evidence of 'Thirteenth Apostle' Found in Israel

Israeli and American archaeologists have discovered what they believe is genuine evidence of a "Thirteenth Apostle" during an excavation near to Jerusalem. The Team led by Dr Chaim Levi of the Department of Antiquities at Haifa University and Dr Julius Goldberger of Nevada State University has discovered an ancient scroll that has been dated from the Ist Century A.D.

"It is in remarkable condition and written in Aramaic. Preliminary translation shows it is the writing of one Carausus Attrebatum who appears to have joined Jesus' followers at the very end of his life," Dr Levi explained. "According to Carausus, he witnessed what other Apostles described as Jesus ascending into heaven. In Carausus' case, he just says he disappeared into a mist. His second name indicates, he was not from the Holy Land at all but from the Attrebates tribes in either Gaul or Roman Britain."

It seems that apart from meeting Jesus, Carausus was one of the very few people to have survived being crucified.

"We have evidence of just a handful of people who survived this dreadful punishment of whom Jesus is the most notable example," Levi explained. " In the case of Carausus and others the task was botched either accidentally or purposefully for a bribe by the executioner. This would have been done by giving him a drug disguised as water that put the recipient into a death-like state before recovering after some hours.

Indeed, some scholars such as John Schonfield have speculated this was how Jesus survived his final ordeal.

Professor Peter Keys the notable British biblical scholar and author of "The Jesus Conundrum" commented: "It is perfectly possible that Carausus was the mysterious Thirteenth Apostle. The fact that none of the Gospels mentions him could merely be because, arriving so late on the scene, he was dismissed as an unimportant observer. But until all Levi and Goldberger's research is complete, the question of whether The Gospel of Carausus is genuine or fake will remain unanswered."

THE ASTROLOGER

Michael Fontaine was not an ordinary mortal. No, he was one of that select and lucky band of modern day Nostradamuses who have the ability to see into all our futures. As the astrologer for Britain's most popular middle range tabloid newspaper *The Sunday Courant* he enjoyed a unique reputation amongst its readership. To them he was quite simply the most perceptive modern seer. He seemed to have the knack of foretelling exactly what would happen to every reader in the coming week be they Aquarius, Cancer or Leo. Needless to say, this inflated reputation far outweighed Michael's actual psychic abilities which were actually nil. In fact, what Michael possessed was a talent with words that enabled him to say absolutely nothing but sound as if he knew everything.

With Taurus in your third aspect (he would write) *you will face a challenging week. Be particularly watchful on Tuesday when travelling to avoid stressful situations. A close friend will test your patience towards the end of the week but maintain your wise Libran counsel. Money matters will feature heavily on Friday and Saturday and it would be as well to exercise caution.*

As his millions of readers would readily testify, Michael Fontaine was indeed correct with all these predictions. Every one of those readers faced a difficult week with many problems both at work and home. Some had conflicts with colleagues, some even lost their jobs whilst others found their sons and daughters had been taking drugs and bunking off school. However, Michael never used negative words such as a problem or conflict, challenging was so much more upbeat and always inferred a positive solution.

Of course, those of his readers who were diagnosed terminally ill faced an especially rigorous challenge to which there was no answer. Unsurprisingly, Michael wisely avoided such difficult subject areas. In his world there was no death and decay, only jam tomorrow. He was also totally correct in warning his avid readers against stressful travel situations. This advice was particularly apt for those many readers facing daily journeys to work in overcrowded trains and congested roads. Similarly, those who had fallen out with a close friend or neighbour over a quite small debt found that, yet again Michael Fontaine was spot on. It did not matter if these readers were Librans, Aquarians, Leos or Geminis, the message was the same for all the star signs. It was just that the words and sentences were in a slightly different order.

Despite his popularity with *The Courant* readership, particularly the females, Michael Fontaine was not liked by those who knew him. Handsome he may have been, with his youthful appearance making him look a good twenty years younger than his fifty-five years, but inside he was a truly ugly man. The truth was that he held the rest of the human race in total disdain, especially those who read his column. He may have been charm itself when appearing on the tv talk shows but elsewhere it was a very different story. At work, he would stride through *The Courant* offices exuding arrogance. If the 'wrong' person approached him he would turn away disdainfully flicking back a quiff of his full blond hair.

Michael had a sense of humour that was superficially funny on first acquaintance. However, this soon palled when one realised it was always at someone else's expense. Everyone desperately hoped this appalling individual would have his comeuppance sooner rather than later. However, nobody envisaged the bizarre fashion this would happen. Under the circumstances, it was as well that Michael Fontaine was not truly clairvoyant. Had he been, his immediate future would have turned his carefully nurtured tan a deathly pale.

Looking down at that insignificant speck of blue dust that was Mother Earth, the gods searched for an agent with which to punish Michael Fontaine for his hubris. In fact, they found an ideal candidate. He was an elderly gentleman with failing eyesight who always crossed Saloman Road, Maidenhead, at the same point and at the same time of the day. Because he had done this for so long without being hit and because he was both stubborn and stupid, he did not look in either direction. The large number of skid marks at this point in Saloman Road bore mute testimony to the near misses the old fool had without ever realising it. However, the Gods had decreed that ten-fifteen on Friday, May 15th, would be different for this lethal member of The Pedestrians Liberation Front.

As he tottered across the road, Michael Fontaine was driving down the same street at nearly fifty miles an hour in his fancy Japanese people carrier. This morning, he was in a state of some agitation. He always liked to be in *The Courant* office early to add the finishing touches to his weekly astrological column and answer the many reader's letters that poured into the newspaper's office. Uncharacteristically, he had overslept and was now in an unholy hurry to reach the station to catch the next train to London.

Reaching down to switch on the radio, Michael's attention was briefly distracted from the road. At that precise moment, the lethal old pedestrian weaved across his path. Returning his attention to the road, he saw the old man directly in front of him. Instinctively, he pulled the wheel over to the right.

Miraculously, he did not hit the pedestrian but brushed his coat. This caused the old man to pirouette gracefully like a ballet dancer. Other than that, he was not directly harmed. However, this was somewhat academic in the general scheme of things. Having pressed him into service to punish Fontaine, the gods decided that the irascible old buffer was dispensable. As he stopped spinning, the octogenarian became conscious of a terrible pain in his chest. A split second later he collapsed suffering a massive fatal heart attack.

Actually, quite a small one would have done the trick, but that was not the way of the gods. They did not maintain their pre-eminent position in the firmament without making doubly sure of things. That was also why two years ago, they had prompted Michael Fontaine to buy the people carrier with the worst safety record of all such vehicles. It's narrowness and height may have given it stylish looks but this made it lethal even in a remotely serious accident. Now, as the vehicle hit the kerb, they congratulated themselves on their foresight.

Michael was not really aware of precisely what was happening at that moment in time. Yes, he could see the surrealistic image of the earth turning on its head. He also had the wonderfully free feeling of flying. The unreality of the situation was enhanced by a total absence of sound. In this brief silence he suddenly recalled what he had written about his own star sign:

"This Friday, Taureans will experience an unexpected challenge when embarking on a journey."

At that moment, the car landed on its roof. The shattering impact crushed the cab, enveloping Michael Fontaine in the total darkness of unconsciousness. The prediction had been dead right.

Twenty-year old Tanya Simpson was not a pretty girl by any means, but her personality sparkled. She also had a brain that was as sharp as a razor. However, because her breasts were a little on the small side and her face did not look like a film star's, all she was offered by the tv companies was the job of a lowly paid researcher.

Fortunately, Peter Starr, the editor of *The Sunday Courant,* saw the potential behind the plain exterior and took her on as a trainee journalist. Six months after graduating in political science at a red brick university, Tanya found herself working on minor news stories, and she was loving it. The fact that she had already made a bit of a name for herself certainly seemed to vindicate the editor's original decision.

One aspect that she did not enjoy about the job was Starr's frequent rages. These would blow up with the suddenness of a tropical squall and were twice as frightening. The man's round face would go an alarming puce colour and a vein could be seen throbbing in his neck as he screamed and yelled at some unfortunate journalist. This Friday morning was no exception and Tanya cowered behind her computer terminal waiting for the storm to die down.

"I'll kill that unreliable, arrogant son of a bitch, just see if I don't!" he screamed. "Where the hell is Fontaine?"

"Doesn't he know we have a paper to put to bed? What the

hell are we going to put in the place of his column a blank space?"

"That'd probably be more valuable than most of his predictions," said George Parker, the senior crime journalist. He was renowned for his fearlessness in the face of both mass murderers and his editor.

"Very bloody funny George," Starr snarled. "Look, if you can't say anything constructive just keep your mouth shut will you?"

"Just trying to lighten things up a bit and stop you having your monthly coronary Peter," George replied calmly. "Bit of a laugh though don't you think? Our resident clairvoyant delayed by unforeseen circumstances."

"If you think it so bloody funny why don't you write the damned column?" the editor snapped.

"Sorry Peter, I'm only good at writing fiction not fact," George replied. "Anyway, Mike'll turn up, he always does. Even if he doesn't you could always run one of his old columns, just juggle the words around a bit and the punters'll never notice."

"Hm, you might have a point there," Starr replied thoughtfully, his face returning to a colour approximating normality. "OK we'll give him five minutes and then we'll put plan B into action."

As if on cue, Peter Starr's p.a. walked over to her boss standing in the middle of the open plan office. Cynthia Burgess had worked for Starr for as long as anyone could remember. Perhaps this had given her an immunity to his terrible rages. An attractive and unflappable woman in her forties, she was the perfect foil to the brilliant but mercurial Starr. However, on this occasion, Cynthia seemed uncharacteristically pale and agitated.

"Mr Starr" - she always called the editor Mr Starr, even when they were in bed together - "Mr Starr, I have just had a call from the Thames Valley Police. It seems that Michael Fontaine has had an accident."

"Trust him to rope the old bill in. I suppose they want us to

"Well the answer's no. If Fontaine's written his car off then he must make his own way here. Besides, he should be using the train like everyone else."

"They didn't phone about that," Cynthia persisted quietly. "They phoned to say that he's in Slough General Hospital on a life support machine. They don't expect him to live and since they couldn't find any living relatives, we were the only address they had."

There was a stunned pause in the office, then the editor spoke again:

"Bloody typical," he said. "OK then we'll put Plan B into action. Now who can we get to do the job?"

As he looked around the office for a likely candidate, his gaze alighted upon Tanya.

"Ah just the person," he said with some relief. "Now Tanya this is a very important little job."

"But I can't Mr Starr!" Tanya protested, her voice edged with panic.

"Why ever not?" Peter asked.

"I'm not a clairvoyant. I don't know the first thing about astrology."

"Don't worry about that," the editor replied. "Nor did Michael!"

She could not help noticing that the editor was already referring to Fontaine in the past tense.

"Come with me," he said and strode across to Fontaine's empty desk and flicked on his computer. "Now all you do is go into his old files, pick a prediction from say ooh this time in 1998, juggle the words around a bit and fling in some bromide about Leo being in the aspect of Pisces, you know the sort of rubbish these *la las* use, everybody does. Then bingo! We have Mystic Mike's latest staggering predictions. Right, I'll give you till lunch time."

With that Starr walked off leaving Tanya staring at the computer screen in desperation and disbelief. After five minutes she had pulled herself together.

Come on Tanya, snap out of it! said her brutal inner self. *Do what the man says and put down any old rubbish. If it all goes pear shaped Fontaine'll get the blame not you and he'll be dead meat.*

Tanya began to type in her predictions, a little hesitantly at first and then with greater confidence. To her amazement, she found she was enjoying herself. By the time she finished the last star, Gemini she thought it was, she did not even bother to refer to Michael's old predictions.

"Hm very good," the editor said as she showed him her handiwork a little over an hour later. He flicked through some more of her work:

"*Very* good. Sure you wouldn't like to do this full time?"

"No thank you Mr Starr," she replied. "I really had my heart set on being a lobby correspondent."

"But Tanya this is much more fun than politics and much more real," Starr persisted.

"No, but thanks all the same," Tanya replied. "Glad I was able to help out in some way."

Meanwhile, Michael Fontaine was floating through a wonderful cloudscape. To his right and left, huge cumulo nimbus thunderheads contrasted brilliantly against the deep blue sky. Suddenly he was conscious of the figure of an old age pensioner in a grey raincoat waving at him with his walking stick. As the figure loomed closer, he realised it was the old man whom he nearly ran over.

"You reckless young bugger!" the pensioner shouted.

"Why don't you just go off and die," Michael replied.

"I already have," the old man shouted back. "You killed me you hooligan! That's why I'm here. How am I going to get my pension now?"

The old man continued to shout and gesticulate as he drifted away behind Michael. He then became aware that he was floating into a large amphitheatre. It seemed to be full of strange and exotic people. Their clothes glowed in vibrant hues of deep reds, blues and greens. Auras of brilliant white light surrounded their golden heads. Michael could have been mistaken but they all seemed to be laughing and pointing at *him*. For such a self-important person this was an irritating and unsettling experience.

"What's so funny?" he asked angrily.

"You are of course," a dismembered voice said with a chuckle.

"How dare you!" Michael shouted indignantly only to be greeted by another wave of laughter by the strange beings in the amphitheatre.

"Michael Fontaine, in life you were a foolish and self-important individual for which you must now pay," the voice rumbled.

"Were, what do you mean *were*?"

"Because you are going through the process that humans call dying."

"Bloody nonsense, there is no such thing as life after death."

"Suit yourself," the voice sighed a little wearily. "In the meantime, look and learn."

Michael was now conscious of being in the Courant's offices. To his horror he saw that awful plain Jane of a trainee sitting at his desk, his sacred place of work.

"Get out of there you little bitch!" he yelled. "How dare you sit at my desk!"

Tanya merely shivered as Michael Fontaine's furious words blew over her as a frigid draft. Mocked and ignored, he really was in hell.

The sun splashed the ochre carpet in the lounge of the Herbert home in Milton Keynes. The sound of the Sunday papers thudding at the front door drew Anne Herbert away from the task of making the first pot of coffee of the day. Clasping the front of her night dress so that she did not expose her cleavage to the neighbours, she knelt down and picked up the wad of papers and wandered back inside. Throwing *The Sunday Telegraph* and *The Sunday Times* on the table, she settled down with *The Sunday Courant*. The heavies could wait for her husband Mark when he returned from work later on.

Computers, she thought contemptuously. Stupid machines and yet they took over the lives of all who encountered them. What, she wondered was so desperately important that needed Mark's presence at the office at half past eight on a Sunday morning? He mumbled some nonsense about sorting a software programme out for a client. She took little notice and cared even less. As she flicked through the paper, Gandalf, their golden retriever whined pitifully in a futile attempt to emotionally blackmail his mistress into taking him for a walk.

Ignoring him, Anne turned to her favourite part of the paper, Michael Fontaine's *"Star Talk"*. Quite why an intelligent and logical atheist like Anne bothered with the astrology column was a matter for the psychologists. However, she was drawn to it as a moth was drawn to a naked candle flame. Ah there it was! Scorpio her star sign:

"You will undergo a truly challenging time emotionally today when you visit your husband's work at Argon Computers unexpectedly. Don't be too surprised to hear what sounds suspiciously like love making coming from the executive suite. Well your crafty old Libran instinct always told you there was something between Mark and his p.a. Carol."

The mug slipped from her fingers to smash on the parquet flooring. Coffee splashed everywhere sending Gandalf yelping for cover. Anne noticed none of this. She was only conscious of those dreadful words of betrayal leaping out at her. She looked away from the paper feeling dizzy. Sparkly black shapes flickered across her vision and her mouth filled with bile.

"Don't be stupid, she told herself. *This is nonsense! You didn't really read that. It's in the newspaper for God's sake! Syndicated words read by millions so how can it relate specifically to me?* Anne took a deep breath and reread her prediction in the

stars. Sure enough, those dreadful sentences of betrayal were still there. She ran upstairs to the bathroom with its jacuzzi and threw up in the stylish Italian ceramic toilet bowl. After some minutes she felt able to stand and splash cold water on her face.

Looking in the mirror, she scrutinised the woman staring back at her. Allowing for the fact that she had no make-up on and had just been sick, she was still beautiful. Yes, there were a few lines around those blue eyes and a few streaks of grey in her copper hair, but that's what happened when you were nearly forty. Mark had always said he never fancied any other woman and she believed him even though he was ten years younger. Then she thought of Carol his p.a. Pert, bright sexy Carol with her flat stomach and proud breasts that Anne would have envied so much if she thought for one moment that the girl was any sort of a threat.

"You bloody fool!" she snarled back at her reflection. "Of course she was a threat! Mark's a prime target with his directorship and preferential share options. How could you be so stupid?"

Cold, hard anger now drove Anne as she made herself up, highlighting her cheeks and eyes in all those subtle tones Mark loved so ... *said* he loved so much. She dressed in the burgundy velvet suit that he had bought her on their last wedding anniversary. Finally, she went to the Edwardian bureau in his office. Taking a large kitchen knife, she levered open that special drawer in the top right-hand corner, the one that he always kept locked. In it was the heavy service revolver that his father had left him. Of course, it was held illegally since the new gun laws had come into place, but Mark had always said he was damned if he would hand it over to be destroyed. He was right, as Anne loaded the weapon with the shiny bullets Mark really was damned.

The phones on *The Courant* switchboard started ringing just after eleven on that Sunday morning By two in the afternoon all lines were permanently busied out as caller after caller, some distraught, some enraged and some delighted, called in to report on the amazing accuracy of Michael Fontaine's latest column.

Worryingly, a significant number of the callers were threatening the paper and its astrologer with some form of legal action. This included a Cabinet Minister well known for his homophobic views who now feared that he would be "outed".

Apparently, the Fontaine column revealed that his lover, a former male prostitute from the Philippines was about to leave him. The poor man did not know about this event in his life. He did not know what was worse, the revelation that he was gay, that he was harbouring an illegal immigrant in his flat or that he read Fontaine's column. Shortly afterwards, the Minister solved the conundrum himself in the form of an overdose mixed with a stiff whiskey.

Tanya was oblivious to all this. She had spent the weekend away in the Farne Islands off the Northumbrian Coast, watching the colonies Guillemots and assorted seabirds vie for space on those rocky outcrops. The first she was aware that anything was wrong was the hushed atmosphere when she arrived at the office on the Monday morning.

It was uncanny because it was a hush that seemed to precede and follow her wherever she went in *The Courant's* offices. She also could not help noticing the way people seemed to be looking at her and whispering to their colleagues as she passed. No sooner had she sat down at her desk than the Editor's p.a. hurried over to her.

"Mr Starr would like to see you right away Tanya," Cynthia said quietly adding "And that really does mean right away."

Tanya followed the older woman into the editor's office with a deep sense of foreboding. What could she have done? Dammit! Peter Starr gestured to Cynthia to leave the room. She left with bad grace and stood at a nearby desk pretending to busy herself with some paperwork.

"What the hell do you mean by this?" the Editor asked, slapping a copy of the Courant down on the table.

"I'm sorry I don't follow you," Tanya said nervously.

"Well just read it!" Starr said angrily. "Try Leo."

Tanya picked up the paper. It was opened on Fontaine's

astrology page.

"You will have a challenging week," Tanya read in a small, nervous voice. "There will be tensions amongst ...."

"Don't treat me like a fool!" Starr shouted angrily. "That's not what it says." He snatched the paper out of her hand and began reading:

"A difficult day Monday when your wife discovers you have plundered the joint savings account. Further problems when she finds incriminating photos of you with secretary Cynthia Burgess. Lucky colour blue"

"It doesn't say that!" Tanya protested.

"Oh no? Well it does from my perspective!" Starr shouted. "What are you up to Tanya? A little blackmail to supplement your wages?"

Tanya was stunned into silence. What could all this mean?

"Well, you're fired."

Miserably the young girl started to leave. However, her path was blocked by a very flustered Cynthia re-entering the room. Whilst Starr had been shouting at her, Tanya had been vaguely conscious of a tableau that had been played out on the other side of the office window. One of the switchboard operators had hurried up and started an animated conversation with the editor's p.a. Now Cynthia was speaking hurriedly to the Editor.

"Mr Starr, the switchboard is being overwhelmed! They are receiving literally hundreds of calls from readers. They are all claiming their stars are predicting exactly what they fear or hope will happen to them."

"This is all your doing," Peter said pointing an accusing finger at Tanya.

"But how could it be? I couldn't tamper with all those thousands of newspapers." Tanya retorted.

"Millions actually," Starr snapped.

"But she's right Mr Starr," Cynthia added.

Starr sank down in his seat, the normally florid face had

gone a nasty grey colour. Without saying a word Cynthia reached into one of the desk draws and took out a tub of pills. She shook two out and handed them to Starr then poured out a cup of water from a chiller in the room.

"I don't understand any of this," he said weakly. "Do you know Cynthia, it even had something about us under *my* star sign."

"And in mine Peter," she replied blushing furiously and using his Christian name for the first time in her life.

"Look Tanya you'd better go home while we sort this mess out," the editor said. His voice was much calmer now and he was leaning his head on one of his hands with his eyes shut.

"Does that mean I'm not fired?" Tanya asked.

"No you're not fired. Just don't write any more astrology columns."

"I did warn you that I wasn't any good at it."

"Believe you me that is not the problem," he replied in a tired voice.

As Tanya walked out through the office, the rest of the staff looked at her in total silence. She glanced nervously from side to side and became aware of one overriding emotion amongst her colleagues. This was a feeling of awe verging on fear as if they were in the presence of an Old Testament Prophet. They had all seen their star signs in the paper and, for the most part, had not liked what they had read.

Tanya felt sick and weak, but her ordeal was not over yet. In the cavernous, high-tech foyer she was accosted by Bernie the obese commissionaire.

"Oh thank you miss, God bless yer," he babbled kissing her hand. "Now I know the missus is all clear we can live again."

She snatched her hand away and backed out through the glass doors nearly falling down the steps. Vaguely she remembered the doorman once mentioning that his wife had some inoperable form of cancer. With a sense of horror, she realised people were beginning to invest her with miraculous powers. What next? *Saint*

Tanya of Docklands?

Walking down the street she paused at *The Quill and Bottle*. Contrary to what the name suggested, this was a new and rather nasty theme pub. However, being the only one within staggering distance of the office it was a regular haunt of Courant staff. Yes, she needed a stiff drink or five she decided, and pushed her way inside.

In one corner, she found George Parker the crime correspondent. Tanya was shocked at his appearance. Gone was all the cynical self-assurance. Seated in front of her was a drunken wreck surrounded by an array of empty spirit glasses. On the table was a copy of The Courant. It was open at Fontaine's astrology page

"Oh well if it isn't The Witch of Endor," he said looking up.

"Look George whatever it says in there, I didn't write it," she said.

"Then who the bloody hell did?" he snarled.

"I don't know, I only wish I did," Tanya said near to tears. She sat down. "What does it say?"

" You mean you don't know what it says? God give me strength!" George read out of the paper:

"A challenging week for you when Karl Kasimir, The Czech Carver breaks out of Broadmoor Maximum Security Hospital to come looking for you. It will require all your Aquarian resourcefulness to persuade him that you did not stitch him up."

"Mad Karl only broke out early this morning. This was written yesterday, so how did you know about it?"

"That's just it George! I didn't. I swear I didn't write any of that," Tanya protested.

"I don't understand what's going on," George said blearily. "All I know is that I'll be chopped liver if that bastard catches up with me."

"Perhaps the police will catch him first."

"Alternatively, you could wave your magic wand and turn him into a pumpkin."

There was an uncomfortable silence when they both

examined their drinks.

"I have to go now, George," Tanya said, writing her address and number on a piece of paper and handing it to him. "If you want to talk just call me."

He nodded his head wearily and tucked the paper in his wallet. Then she slipped guiltily out of the pub. That was the last she or anyone from *The Courant* saw of George Parker. The next day, the police had to use dental records to identify what was left of him. Initially, they were unsure exactly how many bodies had been discovered until his teeth turned up in the fourth dustbin.

Shut away in her bedsit, Tanya was unaware of all this. For two days she just slept in a desperate attempt to escape the nightmare that had enveloped her. She did not dare open a newspaper, listen to the radio or turn on the television. Tanya did not want to be a Messiah or new Nostradamus, she just wanted to be left alone. Unfortunately, the gods had other ideas.

When Mad Karl awoke, he felt better than he had done for a long, long time. Killing that fat journalist had done him the world of good. The voices in his head were not nagging him anymore and the nosebleeds had completely dried up. He was ravenous now, so he walked down to a local pub and ordered a large sirloin steak washed down with a continental lager.

Although his face was all over the newspapers and t.v. screens, nobody in the pub spared Mad Karl a second glance. Long ago during his last spree of mass killing he had learned the art of effective disguise. Keep it totally simple. Anyone on the lookout for the killer would be expecting a hard bullet headed man. With a good wig covering his shaven head and a pair of tinted glasses, Karl was able to melt into the background with little or no effort.

The meal was overpriced but he did not worry because he was not paying. This was on George Parker. Well, *he* had no use for those crisp tenners any more did he? As he pulled the notes out of George's wallet a slip of paper floated to the floor. He picked it up and read Tanya's name and address with a growing sense of excitement. He had not killed a woman for nearly ten years.

The insistent buzz of the doorbell jarred Tanya awake.

"All right I'm coming," she said drowsily as she wandered over to the door. Cautious by nature, Tanya was not in the habit of just opening her door to all comers.

"Who is it?" she shouted peering through the spyglass set in the door. On the other side stood a pleasant bespectacled man. From this perspective, she could not decide if the hair was genuine or not. Something dark seemed to be coming out of the man's right nostril.

"I'm a friend of George," Mad Karl said. "He asked me to call in to see if you're o.k."

"Why didn't he come himself?" she asked suspiciously.
"He, he's sick, that's why he asked me to come," Mad Karl answered. With the voices back in his head he was having increasing difficulty concentrating on what he was saying.

"Well, tell him I'm fine just a little tired," she said. "I'll call round and see him tomorrow."

Karl was a murder junkie and right now was in desperate need of a fix. Surely that stupid girl realised he needed to caress her

"But I must come in," he said wiping the blood away from his nose.

"O.K., just a minute," Tanya backing away from the door.

"Not a minute! Now!" Karl screamed. He had to feel the cold metal slicing her flesh or he would go completely mad.

"Just a minute Karl," she said desperately hunting for her mobile phone.

"How did you know my name was Karl?" he asked.

"I er George told me about you," she said grabbing the phone off the table. Running towards the back window she started to dial 999.

"He told you about me?" Karl shouted trying to be heard above the voices screaming like harpies in his throbbing head.

"Yes, yes he ... he said what a good friend you were," Tanya replied feverishly trying to open the window. There was a tremendous thump and the nasty sound of splintering wood as the door began to give.

"Emergency, what service do you want?" a metallic voice on the phone asked.

"Police," Tanya said. There was another thump and more splintering as the door of the flat began to give way.

"Police emergency. State your name and location."

At that moment the window suddenly opened causing Tanya to lose hold of her mobile phone.

"Hello caller, hello caller," she heard it saying as it fell to the ground fifteen feet below. Desperately Tanya climbed out onto the ledge. As she summoned up courage to jump Mad Karl burst into the room brandishing a huge knife. He lunged towards the terrified girl just as she jumped. The madman managed to catch her arm in a vice-like grip. The red brick of the outside wall filled Tanya's vision as she hit it hard causing her to momentarily lose consciousness.

Coming round a few seconds later, Tanya had the sensation of being hauled upwards by her right arm. She felt very dizzy and there was a terrible aching pain in her head. A warm thick liquid was splashing down on her. Looking upwards she saw Karl leaning out of the window with blood pouring from his nose. Suddenly, the air seemed to be filled with the sounds of sirens. As he hauled her over the window sill Karl raised his knife in readiness to strike down on his victim's neck.

This is it, thought Tanya and awaited her fate. Then the flat was filled with armed police, their weapons pointing at Karl.

"Drop the weapon Now!" someone shouted three times followed by two shots.

Her recollections of what happened next were mercifully rather hazy. Vaguely, she remembered having to step over pools of blood spreading from Karl's lifeless body as a woman police constable escorted her out of the flat. In the street the faces of the crowd were just blur as she was driven away in a police car.

As it accelerated away, she caught a glimpse of newspaper hoarding outside the convenience store at the corner of her road.

The message on it was stark: "Cyber millionaire shot in deadly love triangle."

Tanya decided it would be a very cold day in hell before she ever read another horoscope.

NEMESIS

The old man turned the goblet over in his gloved hands under the cold light of the quartz lamp. His eyes sparkled with greedy excitement as he caressed the surface of the beautifully fashioned cup.

"Hm, seventeenth century if I'm not mistaken," he said in a clipped accent.

"1686 to be precise," the young man replied. Outwardly his tone was confident and friendly but it concealed a deep contempt for the dealer. He felt disgust at the avaricious glow in his cold grey eyes and the way the thin lips moistened with an almost sexual excitement.

Stephen Penhalligon had known Helmut Dagheim for nearly five years now. To the tourists and good burghers of the Belgian town of Ghent, the German was a respectable antiques dealer. His old shop situated in a quiet side street boasted all the accoutrements of a legitimate business. There were the familiar credit card stickers on the window and many fine antiques on display.

Indeed, Dagheim did sell many pieces that were honestly obtained. However, his enterprise had a darker, more secretive side, for he was the most skilful fence in Western Europe. In over thirty years he had shifted millions of pounds worth of stolen property through his quaint little shop. In recent years a significant proportion of this had come from this ruthless young man.

Stephen had been told of the German by his cellmate whilst doing a spell in prison for GBH. His informant was an old fence who had taken a shine to the younger man. Until being caught, he told Stephen, he had done masses of business with Dagheim and never been let down by him. Stephen or Graig Farrar, to use his real name, had the intelligence to recognise a good opportunity when he saw it. This was his first time in jail and he was determined it would also be his last.

Whilst inside he had seen that most of his fellow prisoners were institutionalised no-hopers locked into a treadmill of repeat offending. Their sojourns on the outside world became shorter and their sentences became longer as time went on. Why this happened was no real mystery, of course. Most of the criminals in prison were not especially bright. Craig, on the other hand, had an exceptionally high IQ. He also had a burning ambition never to see the inside of a prison cell for the rest of his life.

The cliché "butter would not melt in his mouth" suited him admirably. He was twenty-eight but looked five years younger. If you saw him in the street you would be forgiven for mistaking him as an employee of an i.t. or investment company. With stylish glasses and a laptop slung over the shoulder of his fashionable suit he looked more like a computer programmer than a criminal.

He acted the part as well, speaking knowledgeably about antiques in immaculate English. To the many rich people he chose to mix with, he was that "charming young antiques specialist". Taking care not to be too specific, he left the impression he had worked with the greatest dealers in London and continental Europe.

However, the truth was somewhat different. Stephen was actually a vicious thug who had reinvented himself. After his spell in prison, he changed his name to Stephen Penhalligon adopting the guise of a freelance antiques dealer. He also went in search of Helmut Dagheim, for Stephen had no more intention of going straight than returning to jail. In the event, he proved to be highly successful at stealing antiques and evading detection.

Dagheim had been very wary of him at first. However, after Stephen's third visit to his shop with yet another valuable item of silverware, Helmut had been won over. The rest, as they say, is history.

"You have a provenance for this Stephen?" Helmut Dagheim asked.

"Is the Pope a Catholic?" Stephen countered. "Of course I do Helmut."

"Yes of course," the dealer replied hurriedly. "In which case I have a number of clients interested in such items. This should achieve a very good price."

No price could ever match what the goblet had cost its legitimate owner. He had been a reclusive East Anglian farmer and he had paid with his life. As with all his victims, Stephen had selected his quarry carefully. He took care to pick an elderly man who lived alone.

It had not been easy though and Stephen had to stalk him for weeks before he achieved a result. However, the effort proved to be well worthwhile. The farmhouse had a veritable hoard of antique silverware. It was a legacy collected over generations that would vanish and disperse overnight.

With the old man and his dog lying dead on the lounge floor, Stephen cleared the farm of its many antiques. The haul was not far short of three hundred thousand pounds worth of goods including the goblet.

The farmer had a bad reputation for hostility to visitors so nobody discovered the crime for three days. Although they launched a massive manhunt, the police were at a loss as usual. Even a reconstruction on Crimewatch did not help, but Stephen found it very entertaining all the same.

As usual, the deal was sixty per cent to Stephen and forty per cent to Helmut. Then, with the shop closed, the two men discussed future trends over a customary glass of cognac.

"High class ecclesiastical items are always in strong demand," Helmut observed.

"Sorry, I don't do pews," Stephen replied. "They're far too bulky."

"No, no, you misunderstand me," the dealer said. "I mean silverware like old communion goblets and crucifixes. I would have thought all those thousands of old churches scattered throughout Britain would contain a few useful items."

"Well Helmut, as you know I do not steal," Stephen replied. "Nevertheless, some of my dealer contacts in London might be able to help."

It was all pure humbug, of course. Stephen Penhalligon was a common or garden thief, and Dagheim was his fence. They both knew it, yet they always persisted in this elaborate verbal charade. It was part game and part wish fulfilment, as if the pretence gave their sordid enterprise legitimacy.

Once back in England, Stephen gave some serious thought to Dagheim's suggestion. Churches *were* a very good potential source of goods, so he decided to do some market research. Like all good strategists, he knew that time spent in reconnaissance was very rarely wasted.

However, he certainly did not wish to draw attention to himself. Dressed anonymously with a series of simple disguises such as spectacles or a wig, Stephen attended numerous services. Funerals were best with mourners too distracted by grief to notice the earnest young man in the back pew.

It did not take long for Stephen to note a sad sign of the times. Many churches, particularly in and around London now had closed circuit t.v. surveillance. The very last thing he wanted was to feature on some television crime programme.

Many were also locked against unwanted intruders. It was obviously time to cast his net wider. His target would be some out-of-the-way church with a three-hundred-year-old silver plate sitting in the vestry. Armed with a hefty guide to English Churches, a good road map and sat nav, he began travelling the length and breadth of the country.

He had to fit these trips in between other jobs, but he did not mind. For him, the churches had become a sort of pet project. Like any collector, he knew the prized and rare item he sought was out there. It just needed time and patience to find it.

Six months later, Stephen finally hit the jackpot. He was travelling over the North Lancashire moors at the time. It was a grey Monday morning and the narrow road was slick with moisture. Suddenly, through the swirling mist he glimpsed the ghostly shape of a small church on a ridge. Seconds later he came upon a narrow road that appeared to lead to the building.

The sign pointing up the lane said Wiseley Edge. For no reason except a hunch, he decided to investigate. Intuitively, Stephen knew this was where he would find his treasure.

The Church was situated a little way up its own unmetalled track. Parking his anonymous blue Volkswagen on the verge, he walked up to the building. As usual, he carried an expensive camera as a prop.

To the rest of the world, he was Craig Sturdevant, a photographer doing a project on ancient churches. He even had some specially printed cards for anyone who challenged him, but they never did.

Walking through the lytch gate, Stephen was struck by the tidiness of the place. The grass around the graves had been mown and the weeds cut back from the ancient headstones. Just beyond the entrance a varnished wooden sign bade visitors welcome to All Saints, Wycherley Edge in gold letters.

"After your visit, please leave this ancient and lovely church as you would like others to find it."

Inside the porch, Stephen paused to consult his English Churches guide. To his bafflement, he could not find any reference to the church in the book. Shrugging, he turned the heavy round handle on the church door. The latch gave with a satisfying clunk and the door creaked inwards.

What he saw inside made Stephen gasp. The altar was laid out with two gold goblets and a fine silver plate. Walking swiftly down the short aisle he checked all three pieces. Sure enough, they were all hallmarked and he was certain the goblets were not less than eighteen carats. Without further ado, he put them all in his rucksack. Stephen was so absorbed in his work that he did not notice one strange omission from the altar layout. There was no crucifix.

As he looked around the rest of the church interior, his attention was caught by a large wall painting. It was the face of a man made completely out of forest greenery. For an ancient wall painting, it seemed to be in very good condition. In fact, the colours were positively vibrant, making the face seem alive. Wherever he went in the church the bright blue eyes seemed to stare unerringly at him. Letting himself into the vestry he found four beautifully crafted candlesticks and yet another heavy silver plate. He placed them carefully in his rucksack. He calculated that this little haul would pay for all the church visits he had made over the months. He could not wait to see the expression on Helmut's face.

As he let himself out of the rear door of the vestry Stephen noticed that the mist had completely cleared. It was also much darker now as if dusk was approaching. That was strange because he had only been in the church for a few minutes so it must still have been mid-morning. He checked his watch but it had stopped at a minute to eleven. Looking up into the cold blue sky, he saw the clouds moving very fast. The thunderheads were billowing and changing as if they were in a time-lapse sequence of a natural history film.

He suddenly felt very cold and started to hurry through the churchyard. It was then that he noticed how overgrown everything now seemed. As he walked through the long, wet grass, his feet became heavier and colder. His progress also slowed whilst the frigid fingers of a deep frost spread upwards through his body.

Finally, he stood, frozen in midstep as the encroaching darkness engulfed him. Snakelike tendrils of ivy began wrapping themselves around his legs. Then with a frenetic rustling, they spread all over his body which had now turned the pale grey colour of ancient stone. In the gloom, Stephen could see other frozen figures similar to himself.

"Now I have something interesting to show you," Paul said as the couple drove up the narrow lane. It was a tight fit and she hoped that they would not meet a tractor coming in the opposite direction. Fortunately, Paul was a very careful and experienced driver.

They were a slightly odd couple, very well suited in some respects but definitely not in others. Hilary could never imagine being married to him and had told him so many times. He still persevered, driving all the way up from the south to spend the weekends with her. How long was it now? Good God nearly five years! She knew she would have to end it soon, but not today, not just yet.

"This is called Wiseley Edge, but in fact the older name is Wytcherley," Paul explained.

"But they mean the same don't they?" Hilary added. "Wise – wytch - witchcraft."

"Exactly," he replied a little miffed at the way she had stolen his thunder. "In fact, wysecraft was the name for the old religion. Then the Christian church wanted the field for itself so they branded all the old shamans as agents of the devil. That was really when witch became a dirty word."

"It certainly is in this part of the world," she said. "With Pendle just over there."

"Ah yes, but this had nothing to do with them," Paul said parking the car at the entrance to the overgrown lane. "The members of the Wiseley Edge Coven were the ones that were not caught."

"You mean there was a coven of witches here as well?" she asked as they walked up the to the ruined church.

"Oh yes. They took over the church when it became redundant and fell into a ruin in the late seventeenth century," Paul explained. "Rumours quickly spread about sabbats and orgies being held here. Very soon the locals avoided the place altogether."

"But how come they were not caught?" she said. "You know how paranoid the authorities were about witches in those days."

"Search me," Paul shrugged. "I suppose it was the same with all those highly placed Russian spies in the fifties and sixties. Everyone was so busy looking for Reds under their beds that they ignored the ones in the corridors of power."

"You mean this was the coven of the ruling class."

"Probably."

They clambered through the gap in the overgrown hedge surrounding the graveyard. The church was now just a shell with its roof missing and only the lower part of the windows still intact.

"Apparently, they did not just worship the Dark One," Paul said. "But also that mysterious God of Fertility, The Green Man. Many churches still have depictions of him in the form of gargoyles in discreet places."

"What are those?" she asked pointing to what appeared to be some ivy-encrusted figures in one corner of the churchyard.

"Ah well, the local legend has it that they are thieves who have been turned to stone," Paul said. "Lured here by promises of great riches only to fall under the curse of The Green Man."

"Shall we go now?" Suddenly she felt very uneasy and wanted to be rid of this place.

"Don't worry," he said as they retraced their steps. "It's pure nonsense, just a legend."

As the couple left the churchyard, neither of them heard Stephen's desperate, silent screams for help. They were drowned out by the sound of moisture dripping from the surrounding trees in their skeletal winter garb.

TESTICLEES

Many years ago, I used to buy aggregates for concrete from a delightfully eccentric man whom I shall call, for the purposes of this narrative, Harry Smith. He owned a smallholding that sat on a valuable seam of river gravel in Hampshire. It was the time of the seventies building boom, so for Harry, this was like having his own mint. Whenever he needed a bit of extra income, he would fire up his ancient digger and pull shingle out of the ground.

For some months I only spoke to him on the telephone. Then I decided it would be polite to pay Harry a personal visit. To reach the hamlet where he lived, you had to travel down a single track lane with high hedgerows. As I drove cautiously round each narrow bend, I fervently hoped I would not encounter a tractor or worse, a combine harvester. Fortunately, I arrived at my destination without incident. Shortly before reaching the farm, the road widened a little and dissected the property so that the farmhouse was on one side and the yard was on the other.

To my surprise, I saw what appeared to be an ancient Greek statue of a man standing in the middle of the yard. Like most such statues it was magnificently proportioned but minus head and limbs.

Harry greeted me at the entrance of his seventeenth century farmhouse. He was a tall man dressed in corduroys and a tweed jacket. With his wiry physique and ruddy complexion he looked much younger than his sixty-five years. He also had an energy and enthusiasm that you would associate with a much younger man. Walking down the narrow hallway we had to squeeze past a vintage car radiator leaning against the wall.

"Had to bring that in here because some gentlemen of the road tried to nick it from the barn where I'm renovating my Riley," he explained.

After a cup of coffee he took me for a tour of his property.

"Tell me Harry, who or what is that?" I asked as we walked past the statue.

"Oh that's Testiclees," he said giving the figure an affectionate pat. The reason for such a nickname was immediately obvious. What the statue lacked in arms or legs was more than compensated by its ample genitalia.

"My son used to run a storage business and Testiclees here was the property of a rich client who lives overseas," Harry explained. "Unfortunately, the business came to grief, so I agreed to look after the statue in the meantime. I must say it does turn people's heads when they drive past."

"The meantime" turned out to be a number of years and I used to bring visitors to show them Harry Smith's well endowed guest.

Eventually, Testiclees vanished leaving the farmyard looking sad and empty. Fearing he had been stolen I asked Harry what had happened.

Apparently, he had recently received a phone call from a man who identified himself as the representative of the statue's owner.

"I understand you are currently caring for my client's statue," the agent explained.

"That's right," Harry replied a little warily.

"Well, since my client is coming back to the UK shortly, the statue must be returned so it can be placed in his new penthouse," the man explained. "Come and collect it when you like," Harry said affably.

"Of course, I shan't be collecting it personally Mr Smith," the agent replied rather huffily. "With such a valuable artefact that is a job for professionals."

"Valuable?" Harry asked with a sinking feeling. "How valuable?"

"What you'd expect of a three thousand-year-old statue of Alexander The Great," the man said. "It's priceless so I hope it has been stored correctly and securely."

"Oh have no fear on that account," Harry said rolling his eyes heavenwards.

No doubt Testiclees now resides in the secure luxury of a Docklands penthouse. However, I wonder if he really prefers the company of merchant bankers to Harry Smith's cows and chickens.

I am afraid Harry's story did not have such a happy ending. Some years later he was killed by a neighbour in a dispute about land. It ended in what was described to me as a "clash of sticks" in a local churchyard. Sadly, Harry came off the worst of that encounter.

It was a tragic and unnecessary end to a colourful and interesting life.

THE JOURNEY

Naked, featherless and blind, the fledgling flapped his embryonic wings. Lying in the nest amidst the debris of his recent hatching, he opened his beak with an instinctive demand for sustenance. A demand that was soon met by his mother thrusting a beak load of insects down his throat before flying off for more food. Always more food was needed.

Three weeks later, the swallow took flight from the nest. No longer naked and helpless, his body was now covered with a protective sheen of feathers. Out over the tree cover changing from green to autumnal brown, the young swallow twisted, turned and dived towards the river where the insect swarms were thickest. This knowledge had been imprinted within his brain by the chemicals of instinct passed on by the genes of his parents.

Hundreds of other swallows flitted and dived above the rippling waters snapping up the dancing insects in an instant. Suddenly, a warning as strong as it was indistinct caused the young bird to make an instantaneous break to the left and right as he flitted for the cover and safety of the foliage on the bank. Not a moment too soon as the larger predator, a hobby, its pointed wings swept back, made a lightning dive for him. Missing the young swallow the hobby soon made good with a slightly slower bird. Just as the swallows were preying on the insects in readiness for their imminent journey, the hobbies preyed on them in the ceaseless search for food. Failure to catch any of the smaller birds would be repaid by starvation.

Days later the young swallow joined thousands of others migrating south. Flying higher than they had ever done, the flock was driven by a group instinct towards the magnetic warmth of the southern sun. High above, a formation of honking geese overtook them in this annual race for survival.

On the ground below, men fought and killed in their own battles for supremacy. Smoke from their war and pillage smeared the autumn sky. The flocks saw nor sensed none of this as ten thousand wings beat in the air. Neither were they aware of the abandoned villas with their torn roofs and their long-horned cows turning feral in the absence of their Roman owners.

Travelling down the Channel and into the greyness of a Biscay storm, the flock was thinned as weaker members succumbed and died, their frozen bodies falling into the storm-flecked sea. The young swallow lived for he was a strong, natural survivor. Flitting in and out of sleep lasting microseconds, the migrating birds crossed the cruelly beautiful white caps of the Pyrenees where countless travellers had perished as did more of their number. The swallows paid them no heed as they flew on into the heat of Iberia and then the Sahara.

Many more would perish over this arid expanse, their tiny corpses unseen by the camel trains passing to the rich markets of the Levant, Greece and Phoenicia.

Finally, the exhausted swallow and his remaining companions arrived at their destination in the Southern African savannah with its vast herds of game from the mighty elephant to the nimble impala. Here, dense clouds of insects danced and swirled over the waters of lakes and rivers. Ample food for the swallows and their new families of demanding chicks. Ample food for the next perilous journey northwards.

Sixteen hundred summers later a distant descendent of that young swallow flew back to the same nesting area by the Thames. Centuries of flood, weather and man had changed the landscape beyond all recognition but this hardy bird knew nothing of this.

Born in Africa this was his first migration to Britain. Instinct took him to the same nesting place where his ancestor had started life. Then it had been beneath the crumbling tiled roof of a deserted Roman villa. Now it would be a nest in the shadow of a TV satellite dish.

He was home, at least until the autumn when the huge natural magnet would pull him inexorably southwards yet again.

THE ROBIN

The robin hopped forward, its head cocked to one side as it regarded him with its dark, fearless beady eyes. Lawrence gently lowered his book, careful not to make any sudden movement that would startle the bird. The robin hopped forward again until it was standing on the grass not more than a couple of feet from his shoe.

A smile gradually creased his gaunt, bearded face. How long had it been since he had smiled? Must have been way back in Cornwall on a day not dissimilar to this one. A bright summer sun burning down from a deep blue sky flecked with fluffy white clouds. Yes, that was it! Cornwall in that golden summer of 1916. He and Will had been swimming down in a sheltered cove near Zennor. He remembered the young farmer's bronzed body, his muscles finely honed by the combination of open air and manual labour. Shortly after that they had made love for the first time in long, rustling grass high above Will Hocking's farm.

He often wondered whether Frieda had ever guessed their secret. If she did, she never said anything, although on occasions he caught her regarding him with a quizzical look in her dark eyes. Who knows, she might even have been grateful to William, for his trysts with the farmer seemed to give an extra energy and passion to their own lovemaking. But with this, the frequency and violence of their rows also increased.

If Frieda had not spied on him and Will, he suspected others may well have done. From their arrival at Zennor, there had been mutterings amongst the locals about "that writer and his German bitch". Lawrence had not been aware of this talk because he never visited the local inn and always kept his distance from the residents. They were mainly labourers and rough types quite unlike the working people of his native Nottingham. Closed minds and closed faces. However, Frieda was more than aware of these hostile whisperings and told him so.

On his rare visits to the village, he noticed the furtive twitching of curtains in cottage windows and the way people crossed the street to avoid him. He simply put it down to the hostility that an isolated community would often show to strangers. However, William Hocking, who lived on the neighbouring farm, was different. From the very beginning, the handsome young farmer showed only openness and friendship to both Lawrence and Frieda. He would give short shrift to any of the locals speaking of Frieda as "Kaiser Bill's whore."

However, even with his friendship, matters did not improve and the ruggedly beautiful Cornish landscape became Lawrence's prison. Walled in by the hostility of the villagers and torn by the competing passions of William and Frieda, Lawrence sought escape in longer and longer walks along the cliffs. It was only there that he felt truly released from his emotional conflicts and the great conflagration now engulfing Europe.

Then his smile faded rapidly as he remembered the dark events that followed. How wrong he had been to think he could escape the insane violence that was claiming millions of lives in the trenches of Flanders!

The wake-up call for the Lawrences came one night when the moon turned the dark sea to glittering silver. From the window of their cottage they watched as the silhouette of a destroyer was engulfed in flames after it was struck by two torpedoes. This was only the first of many sinkings. There would be numerous other victims of the Kaiser's submarines off the Cornish Coast before this conflict ended.

A soft rustling brought him back to the present. Looking down, he saw the robin pecking and scratching the ground in its ceaseless search for food. Then it hopped away, the prize of a worm in its beak.

After that first sinking, it seemed the authorities made a special point of visiting the Lawrences at all times of the day or night. Often they would be awakened in the early hours by the local police constable who would ask them a list of seemingly trivial questions. For example, there was the saga of the kite. Apparently, there had been reports of someone matching Mr Lawrence's description flying a kite near the cottage.

"Are you aware sir that flying a kite is an offence under The

Defence of The Realm Act?"

"I – we possess no such device constable."

The policeman then nodded and ponderously wrote Lawrence's answer in his notebook.

If it was not flying kites, it was suspected bonfires or the use of binoculars and feeding bread to birds. All such activities were forbidden under the suffocating blanket of DORA - The Defence of The Realm Act. Such official visits were apparently always sparked by reports of someone "matching the description" of Lawrence or Frieda indulging in these subversive activities.

Finally, on a chill night in late October there had been an officious rapping on the cottage door. Opening it slowly, Lawrence saw a young man, no more than twenty in an officer's uniform accompanied by two armed soldiers and the local police constable. The officer had a pale, narrow, clean shaven face with a neat moustache. It was quite the opposite of William's glowing and handsome visage.

"Mr Lawrence?" the officer asked in a razor sharp tone the writer did not much care for. "Mr David Herbert Lawrence?"

"Yes," he replied, unable to keep the irritation from his voice.

"I have a warrant issued under The Defence Of The Realm Act."

"Why for God's sake?" Lawrence demanded with a mixture of anger and shock.

"Oh come now Mr Lawrence, I surely do not have to explain to you and your er *German* friend how much hostility you have stirred up by your activities and The Act clearly states:

"No person shall by word of mouth or in writing spread reports likely to cause disaffection or alarm among any of His Majesty's forces or among the civilian population."

"We have never broken any one of the rules under that Act as police constable Trevenan very well knows!"

"I shall return on Thursday at this time when I expect you both to be gone or you will face arrest for suspected espionage," the officer replied coldly. P.C. Trevenan was visibly smirking. In spite of always showing outward respect and politeness, it was clear he had no love of Lawrence and Frieda or their "foreign jungle ways."

Within days, the Lawrences were gone to pursue a restless and nomadic life plagued by ill health and marital turmoil until his death in France one cold March day in 1930.

The robin had returned to continue its restless search for food at Lawrence's feet. How much this humble little bird could teach the base and cruel humans who also inhabited the earth!

That night Lawrence wrote a letter to his old friend Herbert Farjeon who had loaned him this cottage in the little Berkshire village of Pangbourne. He found the people here no more congenial than those of southern Cornwall.

After Lawrence's departure the ageing robin continued its ceaseless quest for food in the garden of Myrtle Cottage. Two months later, an aeon in avian terms, it finally fell victim of a local cat.

The phone was ringing as Liz Baker fought to pull the buggy through the front door of Myrtle Cottage.

"Mrs Baker?"

"Yes, who's speaking?"

"It's Jonathan Bowen of *The Independent* Mrs Baker. You do live at Myrtle Cottage, Pangbourne is that correct?"

"Yes. Look what's all this about?" Liz asked suspiciously. This was beginning to feel like a sales call.

"Er, I'm a journalist for *the Independent* and I wondered if I could come and talk to you about the time D.H. Lawrence lived in Myrtle Cottage."

"Well that is only a local story Mr Bowen, I don't think there's any actual proof he lived here."

"Oh there is now Mrs Baker. You see a letter has just come up for auction in which he talks about his time at your cottage."

When Bowen visited a couple of days later he brought a copy of the letter with him. After the journalist left, Liz placed a chair in the garden where she imagined Lawrence liked to sit and began to read. It was a hot sunny day very similar to the one on which the author penned his missive to Farjeon nearly ninety years

earlier. Liz imagined she could hear his voice with its thin Nottinghamshire accent echo through her head:
"Dear Bertie,

We like Myrtle Cottage – but Pangbourne is repulsive – it sort of smells - women use scent on their clothes and petrol plus river plus pavement plus women - I suffer by the nose. But here in the garden one has peace. Here there's an old very seedy looking shabby old robin who attends me perpetually when I am working in Ros' garden. He reminds me too much of myself. Sending regards to Joan and the Children D.H.Lawrence."

Liz's attention was caught by a faint rustling sound. Looking up she saw a robin fearlessly staring at her not more than a couple of feet from where she was sitting. Like Lawrence's avian companion all those years previously, it was searching for worms. The more things changed, thought Liz, the more they stayed the same.

BITTER AUGUST
Whitchurch-on-Thames, Summer 1940

Bert Higson would always remember that bright hot summer's day. He remembered the freshly picked tomatoes lying blood red in his basket like an omen. Then there was the sound of a small aircraft high in the blue bowl of the sky. Looking up, he could just make out the shape of a single engine plane. By its leisurely speed he knew it was not a fighter.

Since he was a boy, Bert had been mad keen on aircraft and would have joined the RAF if they had let him. But no, they didn't want asthmatics like Bert. However, there was nothing wrong with his eyesight and even at that height he recognised the aircraft as a German Storch spotter. Now the Luftwaffe had driven the RAF from the skies there was no need for it to hurry.

Forgetting all about his tomatoes, Bert hurried to the entrance of the allotments where his bike was propped up against a tree in Muddy Lane. By the time he arrived back at his little cottage in Eastfield Lane his wife Rose was standing anxiously at the gate.

"Oh Bert," she said tearfully. "Mr Churchill's been on the radio. He says the Gerries have invaded along the south coast!"

"Yeah I know gal. I just seen one of their spotter planes above the allotments. No more than we expected was it?"

"But Bert, what are we going to do?" Rose wailed.

"We're going to fight Rose, we always knew that didn't we? What did Winnie say? Fight 'em on the beaches. Well looks like we're going to fight 'em in the High Street as well. Now I'm going to get my rifle and helmet. You better fetch the kids from school."

Just then, the bells of St Mary's began to toll. In the distance came the mournful wail of air raid sirens from the direction of Reading.

As Bert made his way up the High Street, he was joined by Joe Mankin the landlord of The Greyhound. He was already out of breath as he tried to keep up with the other man. Joe would never run away from the Gerries, he'd be out of breath in no time.

The small contingent of Home Guard gathered at the

entrance to the new army camp in Manor Road. They were met by a tall thin man with a shock of dark hair. The flashes on the upper part his shoulders marked him out as a Canadian.

"Captain Joe McGregor, Royal Canadian Fusiliers," he said by way of introduction.

"I'm Captain Emmerson, head of the village home guard," a bespectacled man in his fifties spoke up. "What would you like us to do Captain?"

What indeed? McGregor wondered as he cast his eye along the rank of assorted farm hands and bank clerks. Most had guns of sorts, but he noticed a few just had scythes and pitchforks. Still, he had no doubt they would do their duty when the time came. How many would be alive after the Panzers had crashed through the village?

"Well, I guess you had better take up defensive positions with my men along the river and by the bridge," McGregor said. "That's the direction they'll most likely come."

The invasion of England dubbed Operation Sealion had begun in the early hours of that morning. The main force under the overall command of General Von Rundstedt landed along the coast from Ramsgate in the east to Portsmouth in the west. Although the German 16th Army quickly established a beachhead along the south coast they had soon become bogged down in heavy fighting. Large numbers of German fallschirmjager (parachutists) had landed in Dover and Brighton just after dawn and were now involved in desperate street to street fighting. Both towns were in flames with many buildings reduced to rubble.

Other contingents of the 16th who had landed to the west of Portsmouth had made greater progress having bypassed the main city with her heavy defences. By ten o'clock, they were already to the north of Petersfield as a large group of Panzer tanks and armoured personnel carriers travelled up the A3 trunk road.

By eleven o'clock Bert Higson was hidden in undergrowth close to the toll bridge. Next to him, Dave Smalley, a short sighted farm worker nervously clutched his rifle as he stared intently through the undergrowth. It was no exaggeration to say that Dave irritated Bert beyond belief and today was no exception.

"I got to have a pee."

"Well you better hurry up," Bert murmured crossly. "We can't keep Adolf waiting can we?"

As far as Dave was concerned, they could keep Herr Hitler waiting for the whole of the war.

Just then there was the baleful sound of Stuka dive bombers, followed by the rumble of explosions as they softened up Reading.

"They ours Bert?" Dave asked.

"Oh yes bound to be aren't they?" Bert replied sarcastically. "Probably using the Town Hall for target practice!"

"They wouldn't do that would they?"

The first they knew the Germans had arrived was the low rumble of a diesel engine accompanied by a metallic clanking sound coming from Pangbourne. Suddenly the sound stopped as a volley of shots rang out. Almost immediately this was followed by a roar as the Panzer fired its massive gun. A huge mushroom of smoke, flame and debris billowed above the rooftops of Pangbourne.

"Blimey, some poor so and so's copped it," Bert muttered fearfully.

Then the ominous rumble and clanking began again steadily growing in volume. Soon the whole ground was vibrating as if the very doors of hell were slamming.

Moments later the camouflaged barrel of a Panzer appeared from behind the undergrowth on the Pangbourne side of the bridge. As it grew in length, it turned and the rest of the tank crashed through the bushes on the riverbank by the bridge. The huge tank paused filling the entrance to the bridge. Evil sparkles of flame danced around the tank turret as it fired its machine gun towards Whitchurch. Bert pressed his face into the damp soil as bullets ripped through the summer leaves like angry bees fractions above his head. Suddenly Dave gave a sharp cry followed by an ominous silence. Peering through the grass, Bert could see his twisted body with his glasses half hanging off his bloody face.

As the Panzer had begun to move forward across the bridge,

figures of soldiers in coal scuttle helmets were running along behind using it for cover. A volley of shots broke out from around the tollhouse as a mixed group of home guardsmen and Canadian soldiers opened up with their rifles. But they were not a match for the mighty behemoth grinding towards them.

Bert knew this was the day he would die. Closing his eyes he prayed that Ruth and the kids would somehow come through all this. The Panzer was now nearing the middle of the bridge and paused to take aim with its huge gun.

Then a miracle happened. With a creaking groan that grew into a huge crash, the old toll bridge disintegrated into the river, tipping the huge tank into the Thames. The metal girders and road collapsed, spilling the following soldiers into its waters. As the tank settled into the river with its turret above the surface, its crew began jumping out of the access hatch. The first two men were cut down before the others hastily raised their hands.

The Achilles heel of Operation Sealion was now exposed here as in many thousands of other points along the battlefront. Like so many bridges throughout Britain, the toll bridge was nowhere near strong enough to take the German armaments and had simply collapsed. Similar scenes were being re-enacted along the whole South Coast/South Downs battlefront as bridges and roads collapsed under the huge weight of German tanks and vehicles. Sure, the invaders would replace them in time, but that was one weapon that Von Rundstedt did not have. This advance was to be no rush across flat Russian steppes or Polish plains.

The invasion force had met its nemesis not by massed legions but by Chesterton's *"Rolling English Road."*
I knew no harm of Bonaparte and plenty of the Squire,
And for to fight the Frenchman I did not much desire;
But I did bash their baggonets because they came arrayed
To straighten out the crooked road an English drunkard made,

After that first onward charge had slowed to a halt, Von Rundstedt reluctantly ordered a fighting withdrawal. The routes back to the beaches were littered with burning vehicles and German dead. With Operation Sealion a failure, the Fuehrer turned his attention to his main prize, the invasion and subjugation of Russia.

St Mary's Churchyard, Whitchurch August 1976

Bert and Rose Higson stood side by side in front of the simple gravestone shadowed by the big yew tree. High above them in the hot blue sky a plane growled through a loop the loop. Bert looked up. No it wasn't a Storch spotter this time, but the weather was just as hot as on that fateful day nearly forty years ago. After bowing their heads in a brief prayer, Rose knelt down and placed a bunch of wild flowers on the grave. Then Bert knelt down and read the inscription on the tombstone as he always did every year.:

Sacred to the Memory of David William Smalley 12th January 1922 - 6th August 1940 Who fell near this place in the service of his country.

"Take care of yourself, Dave," Bert said and, as he always did, placed one of his prize-winning tomatoes next to the bunch of wildflowers.

REPORT INTO SPECIAL INSPECTION OF HOGWARTS SCHOOL OF WITCHCRAFT & WIZARDRY BY OFSTED INSPECTORS JUNE 21st 2007

The special inspection of Hogwarts School of Witchcraft and Wizardry in Scotland made by H.M. Inspectors in June 2007 was instituted as a result of a number of concerns raised by a senior member of staff, Professor Severus Snape. These included the educational regime practised at the school, the wellbeing of the students whilst in the care of the school authorities and the suitability of the senior staff including the Head Teacher to run an educational establishment for minors.

Hogwarts school was established many years ago by Professor Albus Dumbledore with the aim of giving gifted but disturbed pre-teen and teenaged children an all round education using revolutionary methods. These methods can best be described as Proactive Educational Necromantic Therapy (P.E.N.T.).

Professor Snape initially contacted Ofsted's London Office in October 2006. He subsequently made three personal visits to the offices with documentary, photographic and video evidence to back up his claims. As a result of this it was decided to have a special "snap" inspection of the school on 21st June 2007. This meant the school was given 24 hours notice of the visit by the two H.M. Inspectors: Mr J.W. Untermensch and Ms P.C. Hubbard.

It has to be said that all the allegations made by Professor Snape were fully confirmed by the inspectors' visit. In addition, a number of environmental, health & safety and animal welfare issues have also been highlighted.

The school itself can only be accessed by a special steam train that has been considered obsolete by the rail authorities since 1960. It was the opinion of the inspectors that this was not only an extremely hazardous mode of transport for minors let alone any other passengers, it was also clear that the engine's emissions left an unacceptably large carbon footprint in the atmosphere.

On arrival at the main building of the school which is housed in a large 15th Century Castle, the Inspectors were also struck by the large numbers of naked flames being utilised as illumination throughout the school particularly in the refectory. In their opinion these represented an extremely high fire hazard as well as creating a dangerous level of carbon and carbon monoxide emissions. When confronted about this the Head of School Professor Albus Dumbledore asserted that this would not happen since all these naked flames were controlled by special magical forces. The Inspectors considered this answer to be both flippant and insulting. Considering his advanced years and many other eccentric beliefs, the Inspectors felt Professor Dumbledore to be totally unsuited for his role as leader and mentor of young children and should be replaced immediately.

Of equal concern was another senior member of staff, Professor Minerva McGonagall who also seemed to hold strange educational ideas. The Inspectors found her use of hypnotic suggestion to control her young charges to be a particularly disturbing departure from standard teaching practice. This involved visually persuading the pupils that she could change into a cat at will (shape shifting). The Inspectors considered this cocktail of age-old superstition and modern hypnotic techniques to be psychologically damaging to impressionable young minds.

Health issues were also raised by the large number wild birds, particularly owls that seemed to be flying freely about the interior of the school. It was the opinion of the Inspectors that this posed a definite avian flu hazard.

Animal welfare issues were also raised by the keeping of a large mutant canine in total confinement. This wretched creature was kept chained in a dark room in one of the school's basements by its owner the school caretaker, a rather hirsute gentleman called Mr Rubeus Hagrid. Mr Hagrid seemed proud of the fact that he was able to control this dog whom he called Fluffy by means of an auditory "cosh".

Finally, H.M. Inspectors recommended that the school game of Quidditch, a form of aerial volleyball to be banned immediately not only on health & safety grounds but because of its excessively confrontational and competitive nature. It was also felt by the

Inspectors that a less aggressive sport such as cricket should be introduced.

In summary, it is the opinion of H.M. Inspectors that Hogawarts is a failing school. Under special measures, it has been agreed that Professor Severus Snape should take over as head teacher and Principal. We have every confidence that he will be able to make Hogwarts fit for purpose in no time at all.

THE GIRL FROM SAXONY

Elise knew that she did not have long to live. The cancer that had ravaged her body was now at an advanced stage. She realised that this was her last opportunity to unburden herself on her son Jeremy. There were many things in her past that he needed to know. Some had been so traumatic she had buried them deep within her subconscious memory. Now, no matter how painful, she must share them with her son.

When Jeremy came upstairs with her breakfast later that morning, she reached out and gripped his hand

"Jeremy darling stay a little while."

"I'm sorry Mum, but I've got to get off to work. We'll talk tonight."

"No, no, that could be too late," Elise insisted. "What I have to say is important."

Reluctantly, her son sat down again. In retrospect, he was very glad he did.

"You know I was born and brought up in Eastern Germany, on a little farm not far from Magdeburg."

"Yes, when you were very young."

"That's right. Well there are things you need to know," Elise said and she began her story……

The Eggert's farm was not large, just a smallholding covering a few hectares. It lay in the fold of a shallow valley in an area of rich farmland in the German district known as Saxony Anhult. Elise's early childhood had been idyllic. Her mother and father took great pains to protect her and her brother from the ugliness of what was happening around them in wartime Germany. Her memories were mostly happy ones of her mother showing the little girl how to milk their only cow or chasing their collie cross Reuter across the fields. Then, on one day in late summer 1942, everything changed with violent suddenness.

Wilhelm Eggert was a gentle man who hated violence. For a

number of years, he had taught philosophy at the University in Magdeburg. When Hitler and the Nazis came to power, he would have no truck with them. He knew them for what they were, swaggering bullies who trampled all in their path. Unlike many of his neighbours, he refused to join the Nazi Party. Even though she was only six at the time, Elise remembered how their neighbour, Mr Wilt had called round to see her father. It was strange because on this visit, old Mr Wilt was not dressed in his usual farm clothes but in some sort of uniform. On his arm was the broken cross symbol that she had seen on flags when they made rare shopping trips to the nearest town. When she asked her dad what the symbol meant, he replied that it was nothing she should bother her head with.

She thought Mr Wilt looked very smart in the uniform and smiled when she greeted him. However, her mother soon ushered her away. It was not long before the two men had raised their voices in anger. After the confrontation, Mr Wilt had stomped angrily away without saying goodbye.

Not long after that, Wilhelm Eggert lost his job at the University. He had been called into the Chancellor's office and given the stark choice: join the Party or lose his position and livelihood. He chose the latter and from then on he and his family eked out a meagre living on the farm. Elise knew that something big had happened because her father was at home all the time and did not go to work anymore. All she knew was that he and her mum would always take care of her no matter what.

From time to time, other men, also in smart uniforms, would come and bang on the door. After talking with her father, they would always leave in an angry mood.

Then came that dark summer's day in 1942. This time there were four men in black uniforms. It was breakfast time when they rapped on the farmhouse door.

"Herr Eggert, I hope you have decided to do the right and sensible thing. You must join the fight for the Fatherland," the leader of the group said. He was a young man in his early twenties with his blond hair cropped very short. He had an arrogant demeanour.

"Well, well, if it isn't Gunther Wilt, the playground bully, your father must be very proud of you," Wilhelm said mockingly.

"You always were a deviant and yid lover Eggert," Wilt snarled back.

"You can call me all the names you like, but I'll never be part of your Party or it's filthy war!"

"Right, I've had enough of this," Wilt shouted. "Outside all of you! Come on the whole family."

The Gestapo officers roughly herded them through the entrance door to stand against the front wall of the farmhouse. Elise's mother was holding her hand so tightly that it hurt. There were no more angry words. Wilt took out a large pistol from its holster and pointed it at her father's head.

The next moment there was a loud bang and Wilhelm's body jerked back against the wall where it left an ugly spray of blood. No sooner had that happened than Wilt and his men were gone, their Mercedes car disappearing in a cloud of dust. Kneeling on the ground, Marie Eggert cradled her dead husband's shattered head in her arms as she wept hysterically. It was a memory that etched itself on Elise's soul forever.

Somehow, Marie Eggert and the children patched their lives back together. As the months turned to years, the skies were often filled with the throbbing roar of aircraft engines. Every night they heard distant explosions and saw an angry glow on the horizon as Magdeburg was pummelled by American bombs.

Then came that memorable day when there were no more bombers or explosions. Peace had finally returned, and the air was alive with birdsong. It was the summer of 1945, and Elise was eleven. This tranquil period did not last, of course. One day, there was a low, menacing rumble, and they could see tanks in the distance moving down the main road. The Russians had arrived.

Over the next three years, things changed radically in their part of Germany. The radio and the one available newspaper *Neues Deutschland,* informed them they now lived in a Workers Democracy. Everyone was equal, and private property was abolished. Elise grew to hate the occupying Russians with their humourlessness and arrogance. However, she hated her fellow Germans who ran to do the Soviets' bidding even more. As time went on, everything, particularly food, became even scarcer. Apparently, it was all for the good of the state and the socialist worker's society.

She and her friend Cristal often fantasised about escaping this drab and repressive society. Cristal, a dark haired girl, was six months older than Elise and the daughter of a neighbouring farming family who remained on good terms with the Eggerts. The two girls had always been the best of friends

These escape plans remained teenage fantasies until 1948 when an event occurred that convinced Elise that she and Cristal really must make a break for freedom. Elise was now an attractive blonde who looked several years older than her actual age of fifteen.

One spring day, a visitor came to the farm who seemed to be strangely familiar. He had filled out quite a bit since she had last seen him and his large stomach only just fitted in his *Volks Polizei* uniform. With a chill of dread, Elise realised she was looking at Gunter Wilt, her father's murderer.

"I am looking for Comrade Eggert," he said haughtily.
"She's not here," Elise replied coldly.

"Ah you're the daughter," Wilt said, his face softening a fraction. "I am Comrade Paul Smidt." He held out his hand but Elise refused to take it. *And you are my father's murderer, you Nazi swine, she wanted to say,* but fear had stolen her tongue.

Like many of his fellow Gestapo members, Gunther Wilt had managed to evade arrest and re-invent himself as a member of the People's Police in the Soviet zone that would soon become the puppet state of East Germany. The uniform and the political creed may be different, but he remained the same old murderous bully.

"Perhaps you would like to come for a meal. We have a good restaurant for our comrades in the People's Police," Gunther said in a sly and lascivious voice

"No, no I want nothing from you," Elise replied as she slammed the door.

"If only we could be friends, life would be much easier for you fraulein," he shouted in a wheedling tone.

Elise stood with her back pressing against the closed door, her whole body shaking with fear and revulsion.

"That bastard Gunther Wilt is back!" she told her friend Cristal later.

"How? Didn't they arrest him after the War?"

"No, somehow he's become a *Vopo* officer and changed his name. Now he's after me!"

"We really have to escape now," Cristal said with finality.

She did not mean immediately. The girls had to plan their escape carefully or it would end in disaster. They spent the next few days hoarding meagre supplies of food for the journey. Cheese and bread were wrapped in cloths hidden in the girls' bedrooms. The only map they had was an old pre-war school atlas. It was far from accurate, but it would have to do.

"Look, here's Stimmelhalt, that's where we are," Cristal said pointing to their little village near the city of Magdeburg. "Our village is just off the main road from Magdeburg to Schoningen in the West. We are only ten kilometres from the border. Ten kilometres from freedom Elise!"

"But the road will be closed now," Elise said in despair.

"Of course it will!" Cristal replied. "We'll just follow it in the nearby fields. My dad had to go to one of the border farms and he said you could see the border from there and it was just a fence."

That was true at that time. In 1948, the situation in Germany was still pretty chaotic. The communist authorities did not have enough manpower to seal the whole border between the two

Germanies.

The haemorrhaging of people escaping from East Germany to the West had not yet become an issue, so the main effort at closing off routes was concentrated in the border towns. Had the girls delayed their escape for another couple of years, it would have been too late. By then, the whole land frontier would be sealed by high fences and death strips sown with mines.

On a clear night a few days later, the two girls started their escape. It was not without some sadness. Because they feared being discovered, they could not tell any of their schoolmates of their plans. More heartbreakingly, they could not even tell their parents or brothers. So, there were no goodbyes except for a pat on the head for Reuter, Elise's beloved old collie cross. As she bade him farewell, he looked up at her and whined softly. It was as if he sensed he would never see her again.

The girls met up at their pre-arranged rendezvous at a barn in a nearby field.

"Ready?" Cristal asked.

"Yes!" Elise replied. Holding hands, they set off across the fields towards the West.

It was nearly dawn by the time they reached the border. The peaceful landscape was soaked in soft, pink light. The fence was just as Cristal had described it with double-stranded barbed wire stretching across the fields into the distance. A metre in front of the fence there was also a large sign with a stark warning:

Achtung! Demarkations Linie 100 m (Warning Demarcation Line 100 metres).

At the sight of this Cristal, who up until then had been their decisive leader, lost her nerve.

"We can't go Elise! They'll kill us!"

It was now the younger girl's turn to be their leader. She had not come all this way just to turn back.

"We have to Cris!" she said with iron in her voice.

"No, we can't. It was a stupid idea anyway."

"This is our one chance for freedom. Either we take it or we live out our lives as slaves to bastards like Gunther. I know what I'm going to choose. Come on!"

With that Elise stood up and ran at a crouch to the border fence. Cristal followed a few seconds later crying quietly.

"Shut up!" Elise hissed.

At the fence, they paused and, looked out across the fields beyond. It appeared so peaceful and innocent, and yet, for all they knew, armed guards were hidden, waiting to shoot escapees. There might also be mines buried beneath the rich brown soil ready to blow their legs off.

Thrusting these dark thoughts to the back of her mind Elise climbed through the fence and set off across the field at a run with her body bent low to avoid detection. She was light so if there were mines perhaps her weight would not be enough to set them off. Seeing her friend running towards the woods in West Germany, Cristal followed fearfully.

The distance they had to cover was the longest in their lives, and they nearly did not make it. A Russian guard was dozing in a small hut that had escaped the girl's notice. Something woke him when the girls were three-quarters of the way across the field. Seeing the two furtive figures, the man shouted and raised his automatic rifle. He fired two rounds in quick succession. Fortunately, the light was bad, and he was a terrible shot.

The two bullets hissed over the girls' heads narrowly missing them. As they vanished into the blessed safety of the woods, they heard his distant command for them to stop. It was voiced more in frustration than anger. Escapees one Russians nil.

They did not stop running for some minutes until they reached another large sign. This one had a different message in four languages:

You are Now Entering the British Sector.

The girls fell into each other's arms sobbing with relief. They had made it!

The late 1940s was a time of mixed fortunes for the West Germans. For those convicted of war crimes, it meant execution or long prison sentences. For the majority, it was a time of discomfort and shortages whilst living in the wreckage of their defeated country.

For others, it was a time of opportunity. These were the budding entrepreneurs who could see far enough ahead to realise things would not always be like this. One day the sun would once again shine on new buildings that would replace the rubble of post war Germany.

Reinhard Gassen was just such an opportunist. Right after the war when he was discharged from a PoW camp near Frankfurt, he did not sit around feeling sorry for himself like many other ex-soldiers. He could already see a chance to make money out of the occupation troops.

For a couple of years, he made a decent living selling booze and fags on the black market. It was quite simple, really: The G.I.s in the American zone had plenty of cigarettes and nylons, whilst the Ivans in the Soviet Zone had sweet Fanny Adams except for lots and lots of cheap vodka. On the other hand, the French had a good supply of perfume and wine. Meanwhile, the Brits, well, they had whisky, didn't they?

In 1947, he used some of the money he had made on the black market to buy a small disused warehouse on the road to Wolfensbuttel. It did not take long for him and some of his mates to convert it into a roadhouse and bar. That was how Rheinhard's Manhattan Bar was born.

With hundreds of free-spending G.I.s at a base just up the road, the name was no coincidence either. When he had a bit more money maybe he would put up one of those neon signs showing a hostess with a tray of cocktails. With his black market booze and free electricity illegally tapped off the grid, profits were good.

Rheinhard always made sure his bar had plenty of attractive hostesses and barmaids for his American customers. Fortunately for him there was no shortage of pretty girls looking for work in those days. That was how Elise and Cristal came his way. When those two young girls came knocking at the back door of the bar, he was facing a minor emergency.

Only that morning he had fired Olga, that troublesome Russian girl for nicking a bottle of Johnny Walker. When he caught her, she said it had been for 'an American Friend' as if that was any sort of an excuse. He was now down a barmaid and here were these two pretty little chicks standing before him. They looked a bit rough to be frank, but behind their underfed appearance, Rheinhard could see potential. The blonde one was particularly promising.

"Where'd you say you were from?" he asked.

"Wolfensbuttel," the girls replied in unison.

"Hmm. Parents know you're here?" he asked dubiously.

"We're orphans, mum and dad were killed in the war," Elise replied.

"And you're both over eighteen are you?"

"Yes."

He knew they were lying of course, but he needed at least one girl immediately, and so what if they were on the run, he wasn't their father.

"Alright, I'll give you a trial. Go and see Lottie inside. She's the tall blonde. She'll sort you out with a bite to eat and some decent clothes."

That was a year ago and since then both Elise and Cristal developed from naïve teenagers into the dual roles of barmaid and hostess. They quickly learned how to handle the loud-mouthed, sex-starved G.I.s with a mixture of friendliness and firmness. If things got out of hand with drunk soldiers, Rheinhard's heavies were always close at hand to sort matters out.

Rheinhard was not a bad boss either. Sure, he tried it on once in a while but he was harmless enough. The bar was also frequented by a number of British servicemen. Overall, Elise preferred them to the GIs. even though they spent less. They had better manners, for a start, and tended to be a bit quieter than the Yanks.

One night a soldier in the uniform of a British N.C.O. came and sat at the bar. She could not put her finger on it, but something about the soldier attracted Elise.

"You know I really fancy that guy," she said to Cristal. "If he asked me out I'd go out with him."

She was not speaking very quietly because she thought the soldier knew little or no German like most Brits.

"My name's Sandy Prior, would you like to come out with me?" the soldier said in perfect German. Elise was too startled to say no. Three weeks later she and Sandy were married. A year later Jeremy was born.

With her story finished, Elise leaned back on the pillow with her eyes closed. The emotional effort of the unburdening had clearly exhausted her.

"You o.k. mum?" Jeremy asked.

"Yes, but now I must sleep," she whispered.

From then on, the dramatic and tragic story of Elise and her father haunted Jeremy's consciousness. Sadly his mother died a few days after that conversation robbing Jeremy of the answers to the many questions her story had thrown up. Where was the family farm in Upper Saxony? What had happened to his grandfather after he was shot? He must be buried somewhere. How had his grandmother, Elise's mother, fared for the rest of her life? Had she been penalised for her daughter's escape? What had happened to that bastard Gunther Wilt? Was he still alive? It was possible. What about her brothers and sisters – his uncles and aunts?

Jeremy would have followed all these questions up. The problem was that life intervened as it always did. It would be another ten years before Jeremy or Jez as his mates called him would chase up his dramatic family story. By that time he was divorced and living with Barbs a cheerful and engaging woman who also had a marriage and two kids behind her.

Jez now ran his own business installing bespoke kitchens in the largely rural county of Oxfordshire. This kept him very busy, meaning he and Barbs did not have much time to themselves. What little spare time they had was spent walking in the lovely countryside surrounding their house. These walks would often end up at The Pheasant, a typical English pub in a nearby Thameside village.

During their visits to this pub they became friendly with David a divorced man in his seventies whose closest companion was Harold, a collie cross dog. Apparently, David was some sort of writer with a few books to his credit.

"They're all self-published of course," David explained. "These days traditional publishers don't want to know you unless you're a WAG or a celebrity chef. So that rules me out as a serious author in most people's eyes. But I don't care, they've given me a great deal of satisfaction even though I've never made a red cent out of any of them!"

Often, the important decisions we make in our lives are sparked by particular events. So it was with Jez and the story his mum told him about her early life. He had often mulled it over in his mind since her death but never done anything other than that. Then, on his forty-fifth birthday, all that changed. He and Barbs had gone down to Weymouth. He was in a reflective mood as they savoured after-dinner drinks at their favourite seafood restaurant.

"Penny for your thoughts babes," Barb said.

"Oh, I was just thinking about my mum," he said turning his wine glass in his hand.

"Yeah, shame she's not here with us," she replied.

"That story of hers about her early life, it keeps coming back to me," he said. "Now I'm a bit older, I really feel I need to do something about finding out more about it. Especially the way Grandad got shot like that."

"Hm. Maybe you should speak to your cousins in Hamburg."

"Not sure they would know very much."

"But your Uncle Wolfgang would," Barbs said. "He'd have all the details about your Mum's life."

"Yes, but I still need to find out things like where my grandfather was born and where he's buried."

Jez suddenly felt helpless. There was so much to find out and he really didn't know where to start.

"Tell you what," Barbs said. "Next time we're in The Pheasant and Dave's there why not ask him? I bet you he could tell you. He knows everything."

That was an exaggeration of course, but at the very least it started Jez on that important journey to the truth about his mother's dramatic early life. A couple of days later when they saw David at The Pheasant, Jez told him his mother's story.

"That's amazing and tragic," David said. "Your grandfather was very brave to stand up to those Nazi bullyboys like that. He really should be remembered for the hero he was."

"How would I find out about his details, where he's buried that sort of thing?"

"Well, you could try the BundesArchiv, The German Federal Archives, I've always found them very useful when researching things," David said. "On second thoughts, what about your family. Didn't you say you had some cousins in Hamburg?"

"Don't forget your Uncle Wolfgang," Barbs added. "He'd know everything about your Mum."

"There you are then, Jez. I'd contact him tomorrow if I were you," David said. "And I mean tomorrow. He won't be around forever, mate. The day after could be too late."

Fortunately, Wolfgang Eggert spoke good English. He was both delighted and surprised to hear from his young nephew in England.

"Jeremy! Now you are Elise's youngest ja? You are well?"

"Very well Uncle Wolf and you?"

"No so bad for my years."

"I'm doing our family story and I need your help."

"Ja, we call it *Familiengeschichte* in German. What you need to know?"

"Well, its really about my mum, about Elise's life when and where she lived in Germany," Jez said hesitantly. He knew he could be treading on the dangerous ground of painful memories. When his question was greeted with a long silence, he was afraid he had lost the old man.

"Uncle Wolf, you still there?" Jez said eventually. His question was greeted with a long sigh down the phone. It seemed to bring with it a tidal wave of emotions.

"*Bad Erinnerungen, gute Erinnerungen,*" Wolfgang said eventually and began muttering in German.

"I'm sorry Uncle, I don't speak German so well. Could you say that in English."

"Many bad er how you say it in English? Thoughts."

"You mean memories," Jez prompted.

"*Ja, ja das stimmt,* memories," Wolfgang replied slowly. "We say *erinnerungen*." This was followed by another long, tired sigh.

"Perhaps Barbs and I could come over and visit for a few days. We could stay in a hotel."

"To Germany? You come here?" the old man asked in surprise.

"Yes, then you could show us the farm where my Grandad rests," Jez said.

"Ah do not expect too much Jeremy. It was long ago and much has changed with the war and *verdammt Kommunisten.*"

"But we would like to see you and our cousins anyway."

"You would be welcome," Wolfgang said.

Since Barbs "had a thing about flying" she and Jez drove to Germany in late August.

His Uncle Wolfgang had spent his life working at Volkswagen in the city of Wolfsburg. Now in his eighties, he was living out his remaining years in a flat in a suburb of that 'company town'.

Despite his age, Wolfgang Eggert was not stooped and held his six foot frame bolt upright. He also had a full head of snowy white hair. He greeted them warmly when he opened the door. Genuine delight at seeing his nephew after so many years lit up his long thin face. His flat was crammed with memorabilia and family photographs. When they entered, they saw a large photo album on the lounge table.

"Germany has changed," he said with a hint of sadness as he poured them coffee. "These days we have many *auslander*, foreigners. Not all good."

"Is Elise's farm far from here Uncle?"

"No, no, it is at Stimmelhalt towards Magdeburg. Perhaps no more than thirty kilometres. But I don't know how much is left now."

Jez did not know what he meant by that. Perhaps the area had been severely damaged during the war. It seemed as if Wolfgang was holding something back, something he did not wish to say. Jez decided not to press the issue.

"We would still like to see it. Have you ever been back?"

Wolfgang simply shook his head.

"Would you come with us? It would be a big help."

"Yes, I could I suppose," he said doubtfully.

The next day they picked Wolfgang up in Jez's van and set out towards Magdeburg.

"Wolfgang seemed especially reserved.

"My grandfather Wilhelm was a teacher in Magdeburg wasn't he?" Jez asked the old man.

"Yes," he replied. Once again, his short answer did not welcome further enquiries.

After a few miles, they came to a large complex of derelict buildings. Stretching away across the country on either side was an area of cleared land about thirty feet wide. Running along the centre the middle distance on both sides, Jez could see watch towers.

"This is the old border with the DDR," Wolfgang said.

So, this was what the Iron Curtain looked like, Jez thought. It was only when you saw it like this, you could imagine what it was really like. Today it was empty land but during the Cold War it would have been filled with armed uniformed men and their dogs. Below ground there would have been the death strip of mines waiting to maim and kill any who were brave or foolhardy enough to chance their luck escaping.

They carried on for a few kilometres until they came to a small road on the right. A signpost with the name Stimmelhalt on it pointed in the direction of the road.

"Turn here," Wolfgang said.

Not more than five hundred metres down the lane they came to an entrance sign with the name Stimmelhalt on it. Jez thought it was strange because there were no houses in this particular village.

"Are we here?" he asked Wolfgang. The old man nodded silently. As they drove further into the village, he could see the foundations of demolished buildings on either side of the road.

"Who did this Uncle, the Nazis?"

"No," he replied with a bitter laugh. "It was Honecker and those DDR bastards. In the 1970s they flattened many villages near the border: Bardoweick, Lenschow, Wahlstorf, Lankow, Mustin and Neuhof."

"Why?" Jez asked. "It doesn't make sense."

"You want communism to make sense?" Wolfgang asked. "They cleared these border villages, like this one, to make a forbidden area to stop the escapers."

Now Jez understood. It was just a bigger cleared area to make it easier to capture or kill escapees. That's why his Uncle had been so secretive and reluctant to visit Elise's old home. He wanted to spare his nephew this horror.

"The farm is this way," Wolfgang said, pointing ahead. A little further along, they came to the old farmhouse or the shell of it.

What was once a fine, half-timbered building was now just four walls with no roof and square holes where the windows had once been. All the whitewash had peeled from the walls, so Jez could not see where his grandfather had been shot, not that he really wanted to.

"I don't like this place," Barbs said shivering.

"I don't like what they've done to it either," Jez replied. He was beginning to wonder if this visit was such a good idea.

"Your grandfather Wilhelm hated the Nazis," Wolfgang explained. "That's why he lost his job at the University. Even after that, they would not leave him alone. Then they shot him here."

"Hey Jez, look at this," Barbs called out. She was standing at one end of the farmhouse wall looking at something on the ground. Jez and Wolfgang walked over and stood by her. On the ground were two plaques lying side by side. They were almost covered by weeds and grass. Jez cleared the foliage away to reveal the inscriptions on them. The first had the word *Reuter* on it with the inscription: *Unser guter und treuer Freund. Oktober 1942*

The second one read:
Wilhelm Eggert Liebevoller Ehemann, Vater und tapferer Mann
21. Juni 1942

Wolfgang translated without being asked:

"This one says *Reuter, A good and true friend,* and this one is your grandfather's grave, and it says he was a loving husband, father and brave man." His voice quivered with emotion as he said the words.

Jez kneeled down and placed his hand on Reuter's stone, and moved the flat of his hand across its surface. So this was the last resting place of that young girl's beloved dog who ran by her side across the summer fields eighty years ago. The dog had only lived a few months after she had gone. Did he pine away or was it simply old age? Jez wondered. He hoped it was the latter. Then he placed his hand on Wilhelm's stone.

"You were a very brave man granddad, you won't be

forgotten, I promise you that."

The trophy stood high in a little alcove in the assembly hall of the school in Magdeburg. The head teacher, a Frau Gisa Wildenau, had received it in a well-padded box a few months ago. She was mystified at first, but the letter, which Jez had gone to some trouble and expense to translate into German, explained everything. The gift was intended as an award to be presented every year to the pupil in the School who had performed an exceptional deed of 'citizenship and humanity.'

The award itself was a fine piece of crystal in the shape of a giant raindrop. In its centre was a red glass rose. The two plaques on the side of the polished wood stand explained in English and German what the glass sculpture represented. The giant raindrop represented the water of life, without which no living thing could exist. The rose represented the life and hope for humanity that grew from it.

The trophy should be known as The Wilhelm Eggert Award.

THE HUNT FOR LA CAMARGO

It was draughty in that great barn which served as George Swaish's Bristol studio. Dorothy Tuckett shivered as her sister helped her into the dress and rubbed her arms to remove the goose pimples. It was a lovely garment designed specially for a dancer with white frills and the lower part billowing out into a wide bottom. Halfway down the dress was separated into eight segments with a flowered border giving the impression of large petals on the head of a flower. They were very careful with the dress, which at 170 years old was fragile and prone to tearing.

It was not hard to see why Dody was one of Frederick George Swaish's favourite models. With her dark auburn hair, liquid brown eyes and elfin face, Dody Tuckett was an enchantingly beautiful 18-year-old. For this painting of the eighteenth century dancer Marie Camargo George felt that she was absolutely right.

"Shall we start?" George asked briskly. In fact, it was an announcement rather than a question. He stood expectantly by his easel a handsome full bearded man in his mid-thirties. As always, he painted in shirt sleeves and never seemed to feel the cold even on this grey October day in 1911.

Swaish's external demeanour was as business-like as ever but this concealed a deep inner turmoil. This painting was probably the most important commission he had ever had. He could hardly believe his luck when he was contacted by Baroness Orczy, the famous author of *"The Scarlet Pimpernel"*.

She was very precise in her requirements. She wanted a romantic, dreamlike painting of *La Camargo* dancing in an eighteenth century classical garden. The style had to be that of Nicolas Lancret who had often painted the celebrated dancer in the 1730s.

Oh, and yes, there had to be musicians! Two at the top of a long sweep of stone steps, a flautist and a violinist with a further musician playing a cello at the side of the steps.

The choice of a dress had certainly not been accidental. It had been lent to George Swaish specifically for this painting by

Edith Craig. In fact, it was the very dress that Marie Camargo had worn for Lancret's paintings. In a letter to Dody's mother thanking her for the return of her dress, she actually refers to it as "*the Camargo dress*".

The daughter of the celebrated Edwardian actress Ellen Terry, Edith "Edy" Craig was a notable actress, theatre director, set and dress designer. A handsome woman, she had a bohemian and unconventional lifestyle. For many years, she was in what her friend George Bernard Shaw described as "a true ménage a trois" with the writer Christopher St. John (formerly Christabel Marshall) and an artist, Clare "Tony" Atwood. Their circle of friends included the writers Virginia Woolf, Vita Sackville-West and Radclyffe Hall.

Whilst Swaish had chosen Dody because of her physical likeness to Camargo, he had another secret reason. It would give him a legitimate excuse to spend plenty of time with her. That would have been easy six months ago, but not now, not with the arrival of the Reverend Claude Stuart Smith on the scene.

The fact that George Swaish loved Dody was a deep, passionate secret that he had admitted to no living person least of all to the girl. So many times he had been on the brink of pouring out his innermost feelings to her only to draw back at the last moment. For the life of him, he could not explain why. Perhaps he felt constrained by the fact that he was nearly twice her age. Perhaps because he himself was married.

Then, this tall Yorkshireman of the cloth came in and swept her from under his nose. To add insult to injury, the Reverend Stuart Smith was the same age as George! Now, they were to be married early in the following year. The deep sense of loss and jealousy the artist felt was like a dark gaping cavern within him.

"Right Dorothy, I want you stand like this," he said using his hand to gently raise her right arm. "And lean your head back," he said lifting her chin with his hand.

"Why George I think you must be cold! Your hands are shaking!" Dody exclaimed playfully. "That's not like you."

"No er I think I have a slight chill," he replied, all too conscious of the unsteadiness in his voice.

"You must take care of yourself," Dody said tenderly.

The painting took a full month with Dody, her head flung back and arms outstretched in a classical dancer's pose having to be ccompletely still for many long, backbreaking hours. George found his three musicians in Dody's two sisters whilst the cello player was a young friend called Kip Shepard who possessed a whimsical sense of humour and a prodigious artistic talent.

Finally, the painting was finished and presented for the Baroness' perusal. She was well pleased.

On 16th February 1912, Claude Stuart Smith and Dorothy Tuckett were married. For a wedding or engagement present George Swaish gave them a small painting called *"The Eve of St Agnes"*. It was a dreamy and ephemeral study of a nude standing in moonlight pouring through a tall window. Presumably, this was inspired by Keats' erotic poem of the same name. In it he describes the rites a young girl performs on the Eve of St Agnes to see whom she will marry. This may have been simply a personal and beautiful gift from a close friend of the couple. On the other hand, Swaish may have been reaching out to his lost love with a subliminal visual message.

Later in the year, *La Camargo* was hung at the summer exhibition of The Royal West of England Academy. Like all of Swaish's works, it was greatly admired and a local photographer was commissioned to take a picture of it. By that time Dody was pregnant with her daughter Miriam who was born on New Year's Day 1913.

As the dark tides of war engulfed Europe, the many characters in this little drama scattered. The friendship between Swaish and the Tuckett family cooled drastically. It was always said that the rift was caused by the artist's pacifism and outright opposition to the war. This was so strong that he refused even to paint camouflage on military vehicles. Apparently the Tuckett family was so shocked at this act of disloyalty to King and Country that they severed all contact with the artist. Sadly, the rift was never mended and Swaish died in Germany in 1931 at the comparatively young age of 52.

As for Dorothy and Claude, it could not be said that their marriage exactly prospered. Sometime after the birth of their daughter, Claude's health began to deteriorate drastically. He would spend the remaining ten years of his life in various sanatoria in a vain attempt to arrest his decline. He died in the Suffolk town of Ipswich in 1924 aged just 44. One of the few photographs of him at that time shows a man at least thirty years older sitting in a wheel chair. His death certificate described the cause of death as lobar pneumonia and empyema.

In spite of his ill health Claude remained as active as possible. In his capacity as secretary of the Church Socialist Society he wrote a number of fire eating tracts about socialism and Christianity. From about 1921 onwards, he regularly preached at St Mary Le Tower in Ipswich where he lived the last few years of his life.

It seems he was also well connected in left wing circles. In 1910 none other than Ramsay MacDonald the future Labour Prime Minister wrote a letter of reference for him to become a Chaplain in a workhouse and infirmary. He also corresponded with Maxim Litvinoff the Ambassador of the new Soviet State about religious freedom in Russia. George Lansbury was also a close friend and wrote a touching letter of condolence to Dody at the time of Claude's death.

Meanwhile Dody remained in Bristol working as a welfare officer at a local chocolate factory. With her parents effectively living separate lives, Miriam had a rather lonely childhood, although she would not remember it as such in later life. For most of that time she was at St Dunstan's School for Girls in Plymouth. Photographs show a beautiful but solemn child staring wanly at the camera.

She did not seem to have spent many school holidays with her mother. Most of the time it was with friends at a large house in Westbury-on-Trim or at Thaxted in Essex. There she stayed with Conrad Noel the local vicar and his wife Miriam. Noel was an ardent socialist. He earned the title "The Red Vicar" after flying the red flag from the church tower.

As for young Kip Shepard, he went on to become the celebrated artist E.H. Shepard who illustrated A.A. Milne's books, the most famous of which was Winnie The Pooh. It always annoyed him that his most remembered work was of "that silly bear." He was justifiably much prouder of his illustrations of Grahame's "The Wind In The Willows". Apparently, his relationship with Milne was very uneasy whilst he and Grahame really hit it off.

The last connection the Tuckett family had with Swaish's painting was that letter from the owner of the magnificent dress, Edith Craig. Dated January 13th 1913 it thanked the Tucketts for returning her dress. Interestingly she refers to it as the "Camargo" dress and describes it as shabby. A straw in the wind perhaps but also a tenuous clue to the dress's true origin.

The photograph of the Camargo painting and the *"Eve of St Agnes"* painting were inherited by my mother. "She wanted you to have these pictures," said my elder brother Edward.

We were standing in my mother Miriam's small dark living room. It was 1994 and mum had just been moved to a nursing home a mile or so from the old market town of Amersham where she had lived for most of her life.

I accepted the pictures with elation tinged with guilt. Whilst I knew that my mother had become too forgetful to care for herself, I felt as if we were doing something disloyal by putting her in a home. Her solicitor had decided that all mum's belongings still in her house would be left with the family members to whom they had been promised in her will. There was the proviso that should she ever return home we would hand back our loot. In reality we all knew this was highly unlikely.

I was familiar with all the paintings and loved them dearly especially one pastoral scene called *"The Snuff Mill"*. The other was the ephemeral nude painting called *"The Eve of St Agnes"*. Time had not dealt kindly with it since George Swaish gave it to my Grandmother Dody in 1910. It had lost its frame and there was a vertical crack running down the painting. Finally, there was a large black and white photograph of Dody in the *La Camargo* painting in her youthful prime in 1911. What, I wondered, had happened to the original?

In 1996 Miriam passed away and in the following ten years, I searched sporadically for *La Camargo* but with no luck. The girl at The Bristol Museum of Art was sympathetic and helpful but had no knowledge of the painting's whereabouts.

Then in early 2007, I struck gold in a most unexpected way. On a shear impulse I typed the name of George Frederick Swaish into an internet search engine. Of the many sites that came up I chose one called Artnet which lists all the latest auction results for paintings of hundreds of artists. There, to my surprise and delight, was the painting of *La Camargo* showing my beautiful grandmother. It was a moment of surprise and excitement that I shall always treasure.

Apparently it was Lot 75 of an auction conducted by Libert et Castor on 7th April 1995 in Paris.

I put this story of art detection together from the letters and papers I also inherited from my dear mother. To the best of my knowledge, all the facts are correct with the exception of Swaish's hidden love for his eighteen-year-old model. That is pure fancy and speculation on my part. I have never believed that Swaish's pacifism was the real reason for his rift with the Tucketts. After all, they were also Christian socialists and pacifists with many family members being Quakers. So it is quite possible that the parting of ways occurred when Mr and Mrs Tuckett discovered the artist's true feelings for their daughter.

My hope that I could run the painting to earth through Libert & Castor would be dashed. In 2008, a French friend tried to contact them on my behalf. She discovered that unfortunately, they are no longer in business. Furthermore, all details of the purchaser of La Camargo are confidential.

I hit a similar cul de sac with the Camargo dress. I had hoped that it was in the collection relating to Edith Craig's mother, Ellen Terry at the actress' former home at Smallhythe in Kent. Sadly, on enquiry, the curator of the collection said they had no record of such a dress.

A friend and I visited the Wallis Art Museum in central

London which has a number of paintings by Nicolas Lancret. One of these is of that daring and unconventional French dancer Marie Camargo. The dress she is wearing is remarkably similar to the Craig dress worn by Dody.

Everyone directly connected with George Swaish's painting is long gone leaving me with an art mystery that I still hope to solve someday. So, like all good detective stories, this one also has an open and ambiguous ending. However, for the moment, the trail is cold.

THE MOTHER LODE

"You can't be serious!" Mark Williams said incredulously. "Nothing?"

Jeanette Ritchie sighed and adjusted her glasses. If she had heard that once in her professional life, she had heard it a million times. As a probate lawyer she seemed to spend her whole working life picking up the shattered remains of people's hopes.

"I'm afraid I am Mark," she replied. "Every penny your mother possessed was left to your cousin George."

"But that can't be right," Mark said almost shouting. "I was her son for goodness sake!"

"I know, but I am afraid the will says…"

"That's not a will!" Mark shouted. "That's a fake!"

Privately, Jeanette was inclined to agree with him. In her experience the worst culprits in probate chicanery were the cousins, nephews and nieces of the deceased. This was a case where the wrong cat had ended up with the cream if she ever saw one.

"You can always contest it of course…"

"Damned right I will!" Mark interrupted angrily.

"But I honestly wouldn't recommend it," she persisted. "You'd only be throwing good money after bad believe me."

An attractive blonde in her late twenties, Jeanette may have looked innocent, but she could smell a legal rat a mile off. The difficulty, as she well knew, was proving it.

"Well if the will is a fake that's no problem surely?"

"But there's no indication that is the case Mark," said Jeanette. "And even if you are right, contesting it, litigation will cost you a fortune."

The middle-aged man in front of her seemed to crumple and collapse like a tired balloon as the awful truth sank in. Mark had never been very careful with money and had failed to provide adequately for his old age. He always fondly imagined that his mother would 'see him right.'

After all, she banked with Coutts and had all those stocks and shares. Now with less than four years to go before retirement on a minuscule pension, he faced a life of penury ending in death.

"What about her house?" he asked hopefully.

"George gets that as well I'm afraid," Jeanette replied

"The little b…." He left the incomplete expletive hanging in the air like a bad smell. There was a brief silence.

"I thought she loved me," he said his voice quivering with self-pity.

"I'm sure she did Mark," Jeanette replied.

"Then why did she leave me with nothing?"

"Well that's not strictly true, she did leave you all her books and papers."

"Oh big deal, a few Agatha Christies and some soppy letters to my dad."

"Well be that as it may they are now yours," Jeanette replied. "And it's quite a collection. You never know there might be something of real value in those papers."

When Mark took delivery of his mother's effects he saw what the lawyer meant. There were nearly a hundred books many of them bound in leather. As for the papers, they filled a wooden clothes chest. After taking a brief look through them he decided they were only fit for a bonfire.

However, for some reason he failed to act on this immediately and pushed the chest into the storage area of his flat. As matters turned out, that was one of the smartest things Mark Williams ever did.

"So your dear old Mum didn't leave you anything," Denise said.

"Feathers," Mark replied disgustedly.

Denise Robbins was twenty-three with hair like liquid jet, a face as fresh as a spring day and a mind like a razor. She had met Mark whilst working on contract in his office. Despite an age difference of nearly thirty years, a close friendship soon developed between them. Mark really cherished Denise's companionship and looked forward to her occasional visits.

"Just a load of old letters and papers," he replied.

"Have you looked through them?" she asked.

"Not properly. They all seem to be syrupy letters to my old man," he said. "I'm going to burn them when I have the time."

"Don't do that!" Denise said in horror. "You never know, there might be something of real value in there."

"I wish," Mark said ruefully.

"Can I have a look?" she asked.

"Sure, be my guest, they're in that clothes chest in the storage area."

"Ah cool, thanks Mark!"

An hour later she reappeared with a blue exercise book in her hands.

"Seen this have you?"

"No what is it?"

"It's your mum's English book."

"So?"

"Well she's written some stories in here and they're really great!"

"OK so she was a bit of a writer where does that take me?" Mark asked impatiently.

"You could probably have them published," Denise said. "At least have a look at them Mark."

"All right I'll flick through them later" he conceded.

"Fine, but read them properly because I shall be setting you questions."

That evening with little of interest on tv, Mark decided to examine his mother's exercise book. It was quite unlike its modern counterparts with a hard cover of Royal Blue. On it the words "St Osyth's School for Girls" was picked out in faded gold lettering. Beneath this was the school motto in Latin: "Nil Desperandum" - Never Despair.

He turned the yellowing pages filled with poems about pet cats and gurgling streams. Then he came to the first story. It was about a Jacobite rebel on the run across a frozen landscape and read like a racy historical novel rather than a ten-year-old's essay:

I glanced at my mud spattered breeches and torn riding cloak. My hand stole fearfully to the tell-tale Jacobite badge on my shoulder...

Mark was hooked and he read on in spite of himself.

The anonymous hero stumbled upon a grimy cottage. Would he find shelter from his pursuers there? To his surprise, Mark discovered he really did care.

As I entered the humble abode I noticed two women cowering by a smouldering fire. Then my ears caught the distant thud of horse's hooves.

"Give me shelter and I promise you will not be harmed!" I pleaded.

For a moment the two women did not move. Then the younger one broke the frozen tableaux and came towards me.

"Quick follow me," she said urgently and led me to a cramped attic. As we stepped into the room three rats scurried into their holes.

"You will be safe here if you remain still and silent," she whispered.

Desperate though my plight was I could not help noticing the pale beauty of her half starved face.

It continued in that vein with the couple inevitably falling in love. Finally, the old woman conveniently died of consumption enabling the couple to elope to Virginia.

There were many similar tales of historic romance. Napoleonic soldiers found love whilst retreating from Moscow and heroic nurses fell for dashing officers injured at Waterloo. There was even a tale of an old desk yielding a seventeenth-century love letter.

"Well, what do you think?" Denise asked on the phone the next day.

"Mum could certainly write I'll give you that," Mark said. "And she also knew how to tell a story, but where does that leave me."

"Since you're too thick to work it out for yourself I'll show you," Denise replied.

The following Saturday she arrived at his flat with a buff manila envelope. From it she took out five leaflets and spread them on the coffee table. They were all about the craft of writing romantic fiction and had titles like: *"How to Make Your Heroes and Heroines Leap from the Page"*. All of them carried the name and logo of a publisher called Red Rose Romance.

"You want me to write a bodice ripper?" Mark asked in disbelief.

"Why not? Your Mum did, so it's probably in the genes," Denise replied.

"But that's…"

"Women's work? Is that what you were going to say?"

"Well yes," he replied a little abashed at being second-guessed so easily.

"You're wrong," Denise said. "It's *money* work. Red Rose pay an advance of fourteen grand for every manuscript they accept for publication. Besides, many of their authors with names like Jessica Lagrange and Mary Havenford are blokes like you."

"I still couldn't do it," he said. "I just wouldn't know where to start."

"You start with your mum's stories in that exercise book," Denise said. "The characters and narratives are already there. All you have to do is flesh them out a bit. Just try it for goodness sake!"

"You're really serious about this aren't you?"

"Too right," she replied. "Don't you see? This is the Mother Lode of your mum's will that'll make you a fortune!"

"But why should you care about that?"

"Because I care a great deal for you as a good friend," Denise said emphatically. "And I don't like the way you're sitting around getting all drunk and maudlin about your cousin George doing you down. It's time to move on and get even. I think that writing one of these arched back and torn dress masterpieces is the way to do it!"

Mark did not believe he could write a romantic novel for one moment, but he was also desperate not to disappoint his friend Denise. Which is why he found himself sitting at his computer with his mother's exercise book on one side.

He chose the story of the fleeing Jacobite. This was risky,

since his only knowledge of the word Jacobite was on the label of a cheap blended whiskey. Oh well he supposed he could fill in the historical details later.

Strangely, once he started, the story took on a life of its own. It was as if his dead mother was dictating to him. When he paused, trying to think of a name for his hero he heard her say: "His name is Rory McCallum and he comes from Meigle. Now get on with it boy!"

How he hated the way she used to call him boy! He resumed typing, angrily hitting the keys. Within two days Mark was amazed to discover that he had written over thirty thousand words but when he told Denise, she seemed unimpressed.

"Not bad, but you need twice that for the romantic novel," she said.

Thanks a bunch for the encouragement, he thought huffily returning to his computer. Four days and a 'sick' from work later he had finally finished the book. Triumphantly, he phoned Denise with the good news.

"I knew you could do it," she replied.

"Nobody likes a clever clogs," he said. "Why don't you come round for supper and I'll cook you spag bol whilst you read my masterpiece."

Unlike many divorced men Mark refused to succumb to the dubious charms of convenience food. Instead, he always cooked with ingredients. His spaghetti Bolognese was a veritable culinary *tour de force* and, in the opinion of Denise, certainly worth dying for.

It took her an hour to read the manuscript impatiently waving away offers of wine and crisps. When she reached the last page she looked up. To his surprise he saw tears in her eyes.

"What do you think?" he asked nervously.

"Bloody brilliant Mark, bloody brilliant," she said softly. "You're a natural. What are you going to call it?"

"Er not sure," he replied. "I thought something like *On Tartan Wings*".

"Tartan what?" she exploded.

"Wings?" he ventured anxiously.

"Mark this is an historical romance not a history of The Scottish Air Force! Tartan wings my foot!"

"Well I don't know," he said in exasperation. "What would you suggest?"

"Something like *The Winds of Love*," she replied. "We are talking romance here."

"I thought we were talking about money."

"Romance first, money later."

"Strange, that sounds like a description of my late unlamented marriage," he replied.

Virginia Claybourn, editor-in-Chief of Red Rose Romances knew a sure-fire romantic winner when she saw one and *Winds of Love* certainly filled that particular bill. It had everything her readers adored: adventure, a fugitive hero falling for a beautiful but penniless girl and romance with just a hint of the S word.

"We like your story Mr Williams and will be sending it for acquisition," she told Mark over the telephone.

"Does that mean you're going to send it back?" he asked in a crestfallen tone.

"No, of course not!" Virginia replied with some irritation. "It means we're acquiring it for publication." She could never suffer fools gladly, even when they were good writers.

"There is just the matter of your nom de plume, the name under which you wish to be published."

"What's wrong with Mark Williams?" he asked.

"In this market, the author always has to be a woman," Virginia replied.

"But that's sexist!" Mark protested.

"Mr Williams are you worried about political correctness or do you wish to make some money? The choice is quite simple you know."

At that point Mark Williams became Marina Maclaren, raven haired author of historical romances. As Denise had correctly predicted, he proved to be a natural when it came to romantic slush.

Over the next twelve months he produced four more novels

including *The Ripple of Love* and *A Blizzard of Dreams*. All of them were published under the proud banner of Red Rose Romances.

In his second year he was so successful, he left his hated job to concentrate on the books. For a cut of the profits Denise became his consultant. In effect, this meant she not only replied to the piles of fan mail but also kept him writing.

Then one spring morning Fate threw Mark a couple of sixes.

"What did you say your cousin's name was?" Denise asked as she riffled through the mail.

"George Ambler," he replied. "Why?"

"This George Ambler?" she asked passing a letter over.

One look at the gold embossed address on the parchment style paper told him that the letter was indeed from his despised cousin.

"Dear Ms Mclaren or perhaps I can call you Marina for I already feel I know you so well through your wonderful novels. I am just writing to say how much happiness they have brought into my life. I would be eternally grateful if we could meet since I feel in my heart of hearts that we have much in common.

I await your reply with anticipation.

Yours sincerely,

George Ambler"

"Well I don't know," Mark said. "First the little swine nicks my inheritance and now he wants to come onto me!"

"But don't you see Mark, that letter could just be a way of getting your mum's money back!" Denise said triumphantly.

"How?" Mark asked.

"Well he hasn't typed it," she replied. "Instead he's written it in long hand as a token of his great esteem for your beauty and intelligence."

"Leave it out!" Mark said in disgust.

"That means we can compare his writing with the signature on your mum's will," Denise continued. "So if a hand writing expert says they are by the same person then we've got him bang to rights!"

The graphologist they picked was a dried-up stick of a man, but he certainly knew his job. After examining the writing on the will and the fan letter for what seemed a very long time, he looked up.

"How much money hangs on this?" he asked.

"At least three or four million," Mark replied.

"Then I would definitely lay hands on the original will," the graphologist said.

"Are you saying the two signatures are by the same person?" Denise asked.

"No, I could never say that with total certainty. But there is a 95 to 99% chance that's the case."

Without delay, Mark made an appointment with Jeanette Ritchie, his lawyer. However, neither she nor the police were very encouraging. Apparently, the evidence was still too flimsy to make a case against George Ambler.

"Well, that's that," Mark said.

"Not quite," Denise replied. "Just because the plod are not interested in taking this further doesn't mean to say that we can't."

"Another cunning plan I suppose?"

"That's right. We're going to lay a little honey trap for your cousin."

George Ambler was a rather short and portly man in his early forties. To disguise this, he always dressed in well-tailored suits and, as a final touch of vanity, died his full head of grey hair dark brown.

Now, as he stood at Marina's front door he felt very nervous. His heart thudded like a fist beating at the wall of his chest and his palms felt damp. Finally, the door opened to reveal a young and attractive woman with long sandy hair flowing over her shoulders. Her light blue dress was sculpted by her petite but well endowed figure.

"Mr Ambler I presume," she said in a husky voice.

"Yes," George said swallowing. "And you must be Miss McLaren."

"Oh do call me Marina," she replied. "Please come in."

He followed her into a spacious living room filled with soft music and sunlight. On an expensive coffee table a bottle of chilled white wine with two glasses was arranged between some candles. She motioned George to sit on a deep leather sofa and draped herself next to him.

"I know I'm not a very typical reader of romances," he began apologetically. "But I find your novels take me away from all the cares and pressures of my everyday life."

Like how to spend a million that's not yours, Mark thought bitterly. Sitting in an adjoining bedroom, he watched the unfolding scene on a small colour monitor. Everything was being captured by a digital camcorder disguised as a security camera.

"I was really flattered by your letter," Marina said softly. "I am sure we are destined to become great friends."

George's heart began to race dangerously.

"In fact, I think you can help me with my next story," Marina continued. "You see it's a thriller set in the world of high finance and I need advice about business. I pride myself on the accuracy of my research. So, I felt a successful businessman like you could help in that respect."

George frowned. For the first time since his arrival a tiny seed of unease began to germinate within his mind. What was the writer of historical romances doing writing a modern day thriller?

"I will help you as much as I can of course," he said cautiously. "Perhaps you had better explain what you had in mind."

"I can do better than that," Marina replied, passing him two sheets of A4. "Here's a synopsis of the story."

As he read the outline George Ambler had a dreadful sense of *déjà vu*. There before his eyes was a description of his own act of duplicity. A seemingly loving nephew inveigles his way into the confidence of a dying aunt. With her corpse still warm, he replaces her will with a skilful forgery and inherits everything. Meanwhile, her son, the true beneficiary, receives nothing.

"This is er very interesting," George said, his mouth so dry that he could hardly form the words.

"Are you all right?" Marina asked. "You look a little pale."

"No, no I'm fine really," he said sipping the chilled wine.

"As you may have guessed, writing a book in the thriller genre is quite a departure for me," she continued. "And I really want make it as realistic as possible. I'm really not sure how to end it."

"I-I don't understand," George stammered. He was beginning to feel very unwell as his heartbeat galloped towards oblivion.

"Do you think it's more realistic for my anti-hero to be caught and pay for his sins or escape scot-free?"

"I really wouldn't know. I have no experience of such matters. Look I must be going."

He rose to his feet unsteadily, black dots swimming before his eyes.

"Oh please don't go," Marina pleaded. "Just read my ending, it's not long. There on the next page."

There were just a few words but they caused an icy draught of fear to flood through George Ambler's body:

Dear George, we have proof that the will is a fake. Love Mark

"What sort of a sick joke is this?" George shouted. "Who the hell are you?"

"The ghost of your long-dead conscience George Ambler," Denise said tearing her wig off.

"Bloody nonsense! You'll never be able to prove anything!" George said making for the door.

"Don't you want to see your signature on mum's will?" Mark said as he stepped in front of him. "It's the same as the one on your fan letter."

"Get out of my way," George shouted barging past his cousin.

Once in the street he turned in what he thought was the direction of his parked car. But the shock of the confrontation had totally disoriented him. Hurrying down the road, he searched in vain for his Mercedes. Chemicals began to flood his brain causing him to hallucinate as his heart approached meltdown. Suddenly, he saw the pale face of his dead aunt peering accusingly through the window of a passing car. A stabbing pain sliced through his chest as the sky darkened. Then George's legs folded under him. He was dead before he hit the pavement.

A few days after George's fatal heart attack the phone rang causing Mark and Denise to jump. Since his cousin's untimely death they had been in an emotional state swinging wildly between elation, guilt and fear of discovery. Because of this the phone was diverted to an answer machine, just to be on the safe side.

"Hello Mark, its Jeanette Ritchie. Pick up the phone if you're there I have something interesting to tell you."

"Well, what goes around comes around," the lawyer said when he had finally switched her onto loudspeak.

"Meaning what?"

"You remember that cousin of yours whom you were so angry about?" Jeanette asked.

"Oh yes, poor old George," Mark said uncertainly.

"Goodness you've changed your tune haven't you?"

"I don't like to think ill of any dead person," Mark replied.

"Especially not in this case," Jeanette said. "It seems he had no close family except you. So, he left his entire fortune worth a couple of million after tax to his favourite writer, a lady called Marina McCallum. Know her do you?"

"I think we have met on the odd occasion," Mark replied.

"Then perhaps it's time you renewed the acquaintance and made an honest woman out of her."

A HARMLESS OLD GIT

It was strange, although Paul Churleigh knew he was sixty-seven, he certainly did not feel his age. As far as he was concerned, he felt as fit and alert as he had been twenty years ago. What a pity others did not see it this way, he thought as he walked towards the bus stop on that misty October day.

Take that neighbour of his for example. The thin and energetic lycra biker who lived a few doors up from Paul. Why, only this morning and he had stopped to talk to him.

"Look, if you ever need anyone to do your shopping," the biker said earnestly. "You know if you have a nasty fall or a cold, just let me know."

"Thank you, that's very kind," Paul replied with an outward smile and inward scowl. "I'll certainly bear it in mind."

Patronising idiot! He thought angrily.

Climbing on board the bus he paused for a moment to sort the change for the fare.

"We need the exact amount granddad," the driver said impatiently pointing a sign below his driving position. "Bloke your age should have a bus pass."

"Thanks for that Sherlock, I'd have been totally lost without those pearls of wisdom," Paul replied as he spilled the coins into the tray.

"Alright grandpa, no need to take that tone," the driver replied defensively.

"I'm not *yours* or anybody else's grandpa," Paul said angrily before striding up the aisle. Choosing a window seat, he sat down placing his briefcase protectively on his knees.

"Finally given up driving then Mr Churleigh," a shrill female voice said. He looked up to see his neighbour, a notorious busybody plumping herself next to him.

"Now what makes you think that Mrs Smith?"

"Well, I just thought you being…."

"Old and knackered? No, I'm not quite ready for the glue factory yet."

"Well no of course not," Mrs Smith said in a flustered tone. "I mean I had an uncle who drove right up into his eighties."

After that, there was a blessed silence for a few minutes. But Mrs Smith was one of those people who could never remain silent for very long.

"Going somewhere interesting are we?" she asked in a tone that suggested he suffered from learning difficulties.

"Not particularly," Paul replied. "Just saving the world for democracy."

"That's nice," she said uneasily. In her book old people should not be using clever words.

Taking care to leave the bus two stops before his destination he walked the last five hundred yards. At the redundant church, he slipped in through the unlocked door. Climbing the stairs to the top of the high tower quite took the wind out of him and he had to rest for a short while. It was a good job he had allowed himself plenty of time.

Opening the briefcase, he removed the high-velocity rifle and assembled it, clicking the stock into place and screwing on the silencer. Once the gun was secure on its mini tripod, Paul adjusted the telescopic sight for a spot five hundred yards up the street. Then he waited.

Right on time, his target came into view. In his Savile Row suit, the stocky man looked more like a businessman than a war criminal with the blood of thousands of innocents on his hands. Why the authorities had granted him indefinite leave to remain was a mystery to Paul.

Never mind, that would be put to rights now. With the man's chest in the cross hairs, he squeezed the trigger.

The police did not spare Paul Churleigh a second glance as their patrol car screamed past him. In all the years he had been doing this work, he had never once been considered a suspect. But then, why should he? After all he was just a harmless old git.

A PORTRAIT OF A LADY

Although not more than two miles, the journey in the little trap seemed much longer than the one he had just made in the train from London. After leaving Medbourne Station, they rattled over a long wooden bridge spanning the slow moving waters of the Thames. Mercifully, there were many trees in the village which provided ample shelter from the scorching summer sun.

However, there was little escape from the chalky dust kicked up from the road. Henry fanned himself with his hat but this provided scant relief. The driver was a large tanned man in his thirties called Ned who used his whip sparingly on the little black horse pulling the cart.

"This yer first visit to Avonwick I'm thinking Mr James?" Ned asked.

"You are correct in that," Henry answered.

"Forgive me askin' but yer not from these parts sir?"

"Like Mr Dane I am from the New World originally," Henry answered with a wry smile. Such curiosity from a servant would have been regarded as impertinent nosiness by many. But as a writer and keen observer of human nature himself Henry James appreciated an enquiring mind no matter which class its owner belonged to.

After they pulled up at the front door of the large Elizabethan house, Ned helped James down and carried his case through the large oak door.

Eliza Dane greeted him in the main hall of the old house.

"Mr James, this is indeed a pleasure," she said holding out a long graceful hand.

"The pleasure is all mine Mrs Dane," he replied kissing the hand lightly.

"Call me Eliza please. How was your journey from the metropolis?" she asked.

"It was pleasant enough," he replied. "But the train compartments are never completely right. Always chilly in winter and too hot in summer."

"Well, you are just in time to slake your thirst for we are having tea on the terrace."

James followed her, admiring the graceful and effortless way she moved. The folds of her long dress rustled like the whispering of river nymphs. However, whilst many men's admiration would have been tinged with hidden lust, his was devoid of sexuality. For Henry admired women in much the same way his host loved his thoroughbreds, without physical desire.

The scene on the terrace of the old house embodied everything that Henry James loved about his adopted country. Ladies in their fine dresses and gentlemen in double-breasted suits attended by servants dispensing tea from a silver service.

"Clarence dear, this is Mr Henry James whom I met at the sculpture exhibition in London," Eliza said to a large man with a long face and full, well trimmed moustache.

"Welcome Mr James, my wife tells me you are making quite a name for yourself as a writer," Sir Clarence Dane said rising and holding his hand out.

"She is most kind Sir Clarence," Henry said. "I try my best of course, but I fear I have some way to go before I reach the dizzy heights of the likes of Dickens."

"You are too modest Henry!" Eliza interjected. "The critics insist Daisy Miller is a masterpiece of comic manners."

How kind she was! He wished he could be as certain as she of the quality of his work. Daisy, was written as a part homage and part exorcism of the unconsummated love he had felt for his beloved cousin Minnie. On numerous occasions in her presence, they had been so close to actual contact, only for him to draw back with the unaccountable horror he felt for the physical side of their romance.

Life and love he thought would be so much simpler if freed from the dreadful shackles of the physical. He had hoped that Minnie would feel this as well, but it seemed as if she were hurt by his drawing back from touching her.

Later, seated in the train back to London, Henry ran the memory of his visit to Avonwick through his mind. The image of the Dane family, the women in their light coloured dresses contrasting the warm stone of the old house and Clarence Dane in his double breasted suit was as vivid as a fine painting. He took out his notebook and began recording the scene in his inimitable prose.

"I trust you will visit us again Henry," Eliza Dane had said to him as they parted.

Indeed, that was the first of a number of visits the writer made to Avonwick over the years. He had incorporated a description of that first tea party in his book Portrait of a Lady with his heroine Isobel having more than a passing physical resemblance to his hostess Eliza Dane.

Partly because of this and partly because of his natural shyness, he held back from presenting her with the first part of his incomplete manuscript. For it was at the very beginning of this that he included a description of the tea party at Avonwick. Finally, on his fourth visit, he gave it to her.

"Why Henry, that is too kind," she said softly.

A month later, he returned, this time for a weekend at the old house. With trepidation he waited for Eliza's reaction to his work. She broached the subject whilst they were walking close to the riverbank. It was a beautiful summer's day with the sun making the grass and trees grow with green life.

"Clarence and I were flattered that you included the old house in your new story," she said.

"I was half afraid you would be offended," he replied.

"Why for goodness sake? It is not every day one appears in the work of a celebrated author."

"And what did you think of the heroine?" he asked cautiously.

"Ah yes poor Isobel Archer, a free spirit pinned to the duties of marriage like a butterfly in a collector's case. You know, I think I see something of myself in that girl," she said looking at James with a mischievous twinkle in her eye.

"But there is no comparison," Henry said hastily. "You are a sophisticate with a successful marriage whereas she is too impetuous ever to find true happiness"

"What becomes of her then?" Eliza asked. "Does she leave that impossible man she has married?"

"Gilbert Osmond? Why I had not decided," he replied fervently hoping she would not ask if he had based Osmond on her husband Clarence. "What do you think she should do?"

"If I were her I would put as much distance between him and myself as possible,"

"But mercifully you are not."

Eliza laughed ruefully and began walking up the long sweep of a lawn towards the old house. Then she paused and looked back at the author.

"Did you glimpse the strange house on the hill as you approached our gates?" she asked.

"The curious building with pointy flintstone towers?"

"It is called The Baulk," Eliza said. "A folly built by my husband for one of his many follies. There are others scattered about."

She moved closer looking straight at him with those disconcerting blue eyes of hers. He did not think he had ever seen her looking more beautiful as the summer sun lit her delicate complexion. It was a beauty that was tinged with great sadness and hurt.

The implication in the word follies left little room for doubt that she was referring to his husband's mistresses. Not just one it would seem but many. How could he with such a beautiful wife?

"You should set your Isabel free," she said leaving her moist lips parted, it seemed to him, in expectation. Like an old demon that fear of female closeness he had felt with cousin Minnie all those years ago returned.

"I will," he said decisively and turned away from her. "But I fear that she will never really find freedom."

"No, I am afraid she will not," Eliza said. James sensed an immense sadness in her voice for he knew that neither of them had been speaking of the American heiress in his story. They walked back towards the house in silence for a while.

"You have never considered marriage Henry?" she asked.

"No, I er have had friendships with ladies in the past but they have never led to matrimony," he said a little hesitantly. Discussing this side of his life always made him feel awkward.

"A pity, I would say."

"We each have to deal with the hand that fate gives us."

Over the next month Henry James completed the manuscript for Portrait of a Lady. Until his last meeting with Eliza Dane he thought he had definitely decided on his heroine's fate. Now the novel ended on a note of uncertainty leaving the reader to decide whether she would abandon her selfish, wanton husband or return out of a sense of marital duty.

After the publication of this novel, James became a less frequent visitor to Avonwick. Eliza was unsure whether this was because of his travels in Europe or whether he found their relationship too fraught and complex. In reality, James was entering an intense phase of his friendship with the prolific American writer Constance Fenimore Woolson. Nobody knows what truly passed between them in private. It is likely that Constance's passionate feelings for the older man were not reciprocated. Despite the torment this caused them both, they remained close friends.

On his infrequent visits to Avonwick, Eliza picked up on the tangled emotional strands of their relationship. However, he came close to revealing the true situation only once. It was on a summer's afternoon in 1889 when they were taking tea together on the veranda at Avonwick.

"How is Constance?" she asked.

"She's well," James replied.

"I hope you can bring her on your next visit. Such a talented writer, I would love to meet her."

"That may be possible next year. She plans to do a grand tour of Egypt and Greece this winter."

"You are such close friends Henry, it seems a pity you can not marry."

"It is that very closeness that drives us apart," he said unsteadily. She noticed his hands were shaking so much, the tea spilled from his bone china cup.

"My dear man are you alright?" she asked with concern etched on her face.

"I am quite well thank you, it is just that subject I find difficulty with."

"Then we shall talk of it no more," Eliza said with finality.

Death would intervene before Henry James could bring Constance Woolson to visit Eliza Dane. In the early winter 1894, she received a distraught letter from James. It seemed that Constance had fallen from the balcony of her apartment overlooking the Grand Canal in Venice sustaining fatal injuries. He gladly accepted her invitation to stay for a few days.

James was fifty-one at the time, but Eliza was shocked by his appearance. He looked much older with his clothes hanging off him and his skin cloaked in a grey pallor. The grief of Constance's sudden and violent death had obviously hit him hard.

"How did it happen Henry, how did she die?" Eliza asked him quietly. They were sitting either side of the great fireplace in Avonwick with its carving of Abraham sacrificing his son Isaac as its centrepiece.

"She fell from her balcony in Venice," he said in a low voice full of pain. "She'd not been well. She was suffering badly from influenza and she was low in spirits. They said she was probably delirious, that's why she fell. I blame myself you know, if only I had been able to show her greater love."

"So it was just a terrible accident," Eliza commented. "You mustn't blame yourself."

"No, it was no accident she, she meant to do it," Henry said covering his face with his hands.

"You don't know that Henry and anyway, even if that were so, it was not your doing."

No matter how hard she tried, he would not be shaken from the belief that Constance's death had been his fault.

By the time he left a few days later, Henry James was in much better shape. The colour had returned to his cheeks replacing the ghastly greyness that had made him appear so old. He also seemed in better spirits, although his manner remained subdued.

Clearly, the tragic death of Constance Fenimore Woolson would remain with him for a long time, probably forever. It was a cold, grey January day when he left Avonwick matching the bleakness of his spirit.

"Come back soon Henry," Eliza said holding his gloved hand.

"I will dearest Eliza, be assured of that," he replied squeezing her hand affectionately.

In spite of that promise, James' visits to Avonwick were very infrequent amounting to only a half dozen over the next few years. During those sojourns, he often seemed distracted. On occasions, his attention seemed to be taken by one of the many upper windows of the old house. It was as if he was seeing people up there.

"Are you sure there are no other guests here?" he would ask her.

"Of course not Henry! I would have told you so if that were the case," Eliza assured him. But he seemed unconvinced.

"I see ghosts everywhere," he once confided in her during a later visit. Perhaps he did. Perhaps he was indeed haunted by the lost spirit of Constance who, unable to possess him in life, pursued him as a lost and lonely spirit from the afterlife.

It was perhaps no coincidence that in 1898, Henry James wrote his unsettling supernatural masterpiece, *The Turn of The Screw*. This tale of an isolated governess confronting two evil, supernatural spirits attempting to possess the children in her charge would cause a sensation when it was published and continue to do so long after his death.

CALLMINDER

Carla sighed with contentment as she negotiated the narrow country lanes in her Porsche. Life was perfect! Well not quite perhaps, but as near as dammit and anyway, wasn't life all about compromise?

Thanks to her husband George she had a really good lifestyle and plenty of friends. It had not always been like that of course. When they were first married fifteen years ago they had really struggled. George was just a lower form of human life in the big finance house where he worked at the time. Then he had struck lucky with all those shares and had the good sense to retire before the dot.com bubble burst.

Now they could look on with equanimity at the scary scenes in the financial markets from the security of their seventeenth century home in Berkshire. They had more than enough money to see them both out in comfort. It would have been good if Carla could tell herself that their marriage was better than ever but she knew that was a lie. As for the sex, well it was best to draw a veil over that!

The trouble was, one's tastes changed and so did one's spouse. One moment you were in love with a man, so desirable you could not have enough of him. The next, you could not care whether you saw him again or not. It had been like that with George. The athletic twenty-five-year old with gorgeous blue eyes had become a middle aged snoring machine.

Still, a Porsche Carrera and home counties pile made up for a great deal, even the lack of lovemaking. Or so she had believed. At first she thought it was her but one look in the mirror told her that was simply not the case. She had a few wrinkles but substantially less than many other thirty-six year old women. With her thick blonde hair and elfin face she bore a strong resemblance to Catherine Deneuve.

It just seemed that George had lost interest in the physical side of things. Mind you, she did not help much, often pleading a headache when he suggested they make love. Eventually, he gave up and now sleeping together meant exactly that.

For a while Carla simply put sex and lovemaking out of her mind. Then she met David at the local theatre group. Almost ten years her junior he was not exactly handsome but had a magnetism about him that she found irresistible. Perhaps it was those dark brown eyes or his enigmatic smile as he cracked another witticism usually at his own expense.

For the first month, she kept her distance at rehearsals or in the pub afterwards. Whenever he offered her a drink she would accept but always bought one in return. Then one evening he made his move.

"Look Carla I know this is an awful cheek, but I've had an invitation to a private view of a friend's paintings and well, I've nobody to come with me. Would you do the honours?"

What harm could there be in a lunchtime view of some mediocre oils? Afterwards he suggested they call back at his flat for a coffee. She accepted knowing full well the visit would not simply end there. From that first passionate encounter they were both hooked and would meet at least twice a week.

Initially, Carla felt terrible spasms of guilt about George. But this only seemed to add life to the affair. Then, realising her husband had no inkling of what was going on she told herself it was OK. After all, if he never *knew* anything was amiss he could not be hurt. In fact, she was sure that her affair with David had actually improved their marriage making her a more attentive and caring partner. Yes, she was actually performing a social service!

Then something strange began to happen. The longer Carla saw David, the more she missed George. She did not understand why this was happening at first. After all David *was* good company and a superb lover. However, after about six months cracks began to appear in his outward façade.

His conversation which always seemed so witty when she

first met him was actually shallow and banal. Even his generosity of spirit was a sham. For example, those humorous anecdotes which he initially told against himself were now turned against other members of the group. In doing so, he seemed to be trying to separate Carla from her friends. When they went for a drink these days, it was usually on their own. If she suggested they spent time with the drama group he would become quite angry

"Oh lets not bother with those boring people," he said tetchily.

"David how can you say that! They're our friends."

"Yours perhaps but never mine!"

From that moment, the countdown to the end of their relationship began. They no longer went out but would meet in his flat. Instead of making love they had sex, mechanical and devoid of feeling. His initial gentleness had turned into brutal physicality. When she reached an orgasm, it left her feeling conquered and despoiled.

Earlier she had her last such squalid encounter and stormed out of David's flat with insults ringing in her ears. Now she was free! Free to start a new life with dear dependable George. The recent past had simply been a secret aberration about which he knew nothing. No harm done. She hummed as she drove home from David with slanting rays of the afternoon sun flickering through the hedgerows.

"Hello sweetie," George greeted her as she walked into the lounge.

"Hello darling," she said brushing his cheek with a chaste kiss. "Had a good day?"

"Yes," he replied. "I have actually. This morning I went for a long walk by Brydon Copse and saw a deer and a woodpecker."

"Wonderful!" she enthused.

"And this afternoon, I set up the new speakers so that we can have music throughout the whole house."

"So we can make love to the sound of Beethoven," she said

moving over and slipping her arms around his neck. Was it her imagination or did his body stiffen momentarily?

"Yes, I suppose we could," he said wistfully and moved away from her.

"Let's try it out now then," Carla said.

"Now?" he said in a startled tone. "Why now?"

"Why not?"

"Because we …. We haven't done anything like that for …."

"Too long George, I know and it's all my fault. Oh, dearest George it's all my fault. I do love you."

"Do you Carla? Do you really love me?"

"Yes!" she replied emphatically. "I really *do* love you George."

With a shock she realised she meant every word.

"I'll be upstairs," she said quietly.

"OK, I'll put the music on," he said.

As she lay on the huge bed, she heard the speakers come life with a soft background hiss. What music would he put on she wondered? Mozart's *'Elvira Madigan'* perhaps or Beethoven's *Ode To Joy*. Knowing George it would be neither of those but Jane Birkin's orgasmic *Je t'aime* with her lover Serge Gainsborg.

Instead, her erotic reverie was broken by an antiseptic female voice.

"First new message. You were called at twelve o'five today:"

There was a short silence followed by a clatter then the sound of someone panting in excitement and gasping out the words: *"Oh, oh oh! Yes! Yes! Yes!!!"*

The voice had a horribly familiar ring to it. Ice began to form in Carla's veins.

"Oh God, Oh David aaaah!"

Yes, it was her voice. But how on earth had George recorded it? Her mobile, it was her mobile! She leapt off the bed and scrabbled in her bag but it wasn't there. She remembered now, she always put it on the side table when they made love.

"Tell me, did the earth move for you?"

She looked up to see George standing in the doorway. The expression on his face was one of pity mingled with disgust.

"Look, George, I can explain," she said desperately.

"Spare me the clichés."

"But I don't understand."

"It's not rocket science," he replied. "In the height of passion you must have knocked your mobile. As it hit the floor it must have triggered the speed dial for our number. Since I wasn't in, it was faithfully recorded by the Callminder lady. I just hope she wasn't too shocked. When I came in I picked it up when I dialled 1571."

"I'm so very sorry George," she said. "So very, very sorry."

"So am I Carla." He replied in a tired voice.

"It's finished George, I promise you!"

"So what was that once more for old times sake? Now perhaps you could pack. The agents are coming to look at the place tomorrow and I'd like you gone before then."

The room suddenly felt cold making Carla shiver. She pulled a dressing gown over her naked body. As she did so the strains of a familiar and haunting song came over the speakers. Carla remembered how she and George danced to it on the very first night they met. It was *You've Lost That Lovin' Feeling* by the Righteous Brothers.

Tears welled up in her eyes and she began to sob. Downstairs George let himself out of the house closing the door with a final click.

THE MAN WITH HEALING HANDS

The little girl standing at the door of his cottage could not have been more than six. Tears were streaming down her face. He recognised her, she was the daughter of Mary Wilkins, the post mistress.

"It's Lizzie isn't it?" he asked. The girl nodded.

"Oh please Mr Bennet, my mum said you could help, you being so good with wild things."

"With what child?" he asked.

She held up her cupped hands to show him a small fledging. It could not have been more than a few days old.

"I think it fell out of a nest," the girl said.

"Yes, I think you are right," he replied gently taking the small creature. "I'll do what I can, but I can't promise anything."

"Thanks ever so much Mr Bennet," the girl said and skipped off down the path.

Since he had come to the village five years previously, he had earned a reputation of being a skilled natural vet who had nursed scores of wild animals back from death. That was why the villagers called him The Man With Healing Hands.

With that little bird, the gentle Mr Bennett was as good as his reputation. He repaired its damaged wing and within a week it was strong enough to fly. On a fine spring morning he opened his front door and released it. As it flew off into the distance, a black Humber car pulled up outside his cottage. Two men in belted coats got out and walked up the path.

"Mr Bennet?" One of them asked.

"Yes?"

"Or should I say Dr Gerhard Bensheim?" the man asked. "Come with us sir. Don't make a fuss will you."

Time had run out for the man they called Dr Death in the camps.

FLYING FOREVER

"Is it how you thought it would be?"

India frowned, the photographer's question was an intrusion, breaking the peace of a special moment. She wished she had not brought him now.

"Yes and no," she replied. "Look Ollie would you mind awfully if you took a walk, I'd like to be on my own here for a little while."

"Sure India, whatever, take all the time you need." With that, he wandered off across the low lying sandy scrub of the island firing off shots at the seabirds as if his Nikon was a weapon.

So here she was on Howland Island at last to pay homage to Amelia. In front of her was all that was left of the crumbling circular navigation beacon. They called it Earhart Light as a tribute. Well, there was not much of it left and it really was not much of a monument. India walked up to the base of the tower and placed the wreath she had brought with her as a special tribute to one of the greatest female aviators who had ever lived and died.

Amelia Earhart had no grave. All anyone knew was that she and her co-pilot Fred Noonan had disappeared with their Lockheed Electra into the vastness of the Pacific close to this sliver of coral thousands of miles from anywhere.

It had cost India Fisher quite a few thousand to get here, but she did not care. It was just, well something that had to be done as thanks to Amelia and her blessed inspiration. Not that Ivan, her partner had the remotest understanding of that.

"I simply don't get it," he had said, his glasses flashing angrily as he jerked his head and hands this way and that. "You're going to spend all those thousands to go to a piece of coral scrub in the middle of the Pacific!"

"It's a pilgrimage," she said wearily for the umpteenth time. "Homage to a great female aviatrix."

"But she's not even buried there is she?" Ivan retorted. "Her remains are somewhere out in the ocean."

"Well, I'm going whether you like it or not," India said with finality. "Anyway, it's my money I'm spending, not yours."

"As you never cease to remind me," Ivan replied with quiet bitterness.

That was, to use the old, old cliche, the last straw. She had known for a long time that her relationship with Ivan had burned out. When she first met him, she had been drawn in by his intensity and sexual magnetism. Yes, to start with it had been very intense both intellectually and physically. However, after six months or so she realised all that was simply a camouflage for his need to control and dominate her.

She well remembered her last words to him as she left to catch the airport taxi.

"I'm off now Ivan," she called pausing at the front door.

"Take care," he said walking through from the lounge. "It's a long way and could be dangerous. We'll talk when you get back."

There was a hint of real concern in his voice that almost made her flunk what she said next. But her mind was made up.

"No, Ivan, that's not going to happen. I want you packed and out of here by the weekend." It was gratifying to see the shock register on his face.

"But India...."

"No buts Ivan, I don't want to see any trace of you when I get back. OK?

"We have to talk about this?" He protested lamely, but he knew his time was up.

"Don't forget to leave the keys on the side," she said closing the door on this latest turbulent episode of her life.

India Fisher was a very unusual woman. Pushing towards her mid forties, she still held onto her striking good looks. She had blonde hair that flowed down to her shoulders, full lips and eyes of blue crystal. Men invariably were bowled over when they met her. However, it was not only her physical attractiveness that made her remarkable but her fierce determination to succeed in a world where men thought they ruled supreme. For she was undoubtedly the best woman pilot in the world.

Like her all time heroine Amelia Earhart, she had been

smitten by aircraft and flying since her early teens. In view of this, it was fortunate that she was heiress to the Fisher Industrial empire. By the time she was eighteen, she not only had her private pilot's licence but also her own plane. It was not any old plane either but a gorgeous bright yellow Boeing Stearman Model 75 biplane beloved by all wing walkers and air display enthusiasts.

In 2010 when she was just twenty, her parents had been killed in a plane crash that had eerie echoes of her idol's fate in 1937. The Lear jet which was taking them to Lake Titicaca simply vanished somewhere over the Andes. No wreckage, no bodies, nothing. It was as if the aircraft and her parents had never existed. India loved her parents and their sudden loss left her devastated, but it also left her heir to a multi billion dollar fortune.

"Mum, Dad, I promise I'll make you proud."

Indeed, she had lived up to that promise she made at their commemoration service. With a host of aviation awards, accolades and prizes she was undoubtedly at the peak of her career as an aviatrix. Sadly, the same could not be said of her private life. That had involved a succession of relationships, none of which had lasted. They were all worn out by the furious and driven pace of her life. Ivan Tierney was just the latest casualty.

Now, here she was on this remote and rather bleak Pacific Atoll, the fierce sun blazing down on her head and a host of seabirds wheeling and screeching in the deep blue bowl of the sky above. She knelt down in front of the wreath she had laid. A crab, startled by her movement, scuttled away into the hot sandy scrub.

"Oh, Amelia, it shouldn't have ended like that for you."

"Bad radio, bad luck, bad place," whispered a voice. Or was it just her imagination moulding the wind into words?

"Glad you came. It gets kinda lonesome round here after all this time." Yes it was definitely voice, a female American voice.

"Amelia?" India asked in disbelief.

"That's me honey."

"So you weren't captured and killed by the Japanese then?"

"Nah, those were fairy tales dreamed up by reporters. We just ran out of gas looking for that little old island. Hit the sea and drowned. Picking Howland for our refuelling point was just dumb. Too small, too easy to miss."

"You were the reason I became a flyer Amelia. You have been the guiding light for my whole life."

"Better flier than lover."

"Sadly, yes"

"Just keep flying honey. Fly forever, that's all that counts." India felt a hand stroke her cheek at that point. A farewell gesture perhaps?

"India, the Captain of the plane says we really have to go." It was Ollie, the photographer again, disturbing her quiet little world.

"How long have I been here?" She asked.

"A good hour and a half. Have you been asleep?"

As they walked back to the lagoon where the flying boat bobbed gently in the azure water, she could see the Captain and navigator waiting impatiently by the dingy on the shoreline. She could hardly blame them. This area had a nasty reputation for the weather suddenly turning stormy and vicious.

"We really should be leaving Miss Fisher," the pilot said to her as he helped her into the dingy. "There's some bad weather blowing in from the North."

"Remind me to tell you about the electric storm I flew through above the Andaman Sea," she replied by way of a rebuke.

"I know your reputation as a pilot Miss Fisher, which is why you'll understand the urgency," the pilot replied.

"OK Captain you're the boss," India replied. "Let's go."

As the flying boat lifted off from the sea leaving a creamy wake, India was sure she heard Amelia's voice above the whine of the turbo props.

"Keep flying India, don't stop, keep flying forever."

ESCAPE FROM ROOM 101

Police Sergeant Daly looked at the man behind the two-way mirror with curiosity. Dressed in a grey set of overalls, he was thin and undernourished. His face, with its sunken cheeks had a haunted look to it. Here was a person who had spent their life walking in fear of greater authority exposing and accusing him, but of what? His dress and demeanour seemed to speak of another time and place entirely.

"Where did you pick this one up then?" he asked PC Jane Foster quietly.

"The Spotted Hen Sarge, in Whitchurch, he tried to pay for his drink with some wacky money that I've never seen before."

'He's an odd one alright. Who wanders around dressed in 1950s overalls these days?"

Daly was right of course. Sitting in the interrogation room was the original refugee, a displaced person from another age entirely.

How had it happened? One moment Winston Smith was being dragged back into Room 101 shaking in fear at the thought of confronting those frenzied rats again. The next moment he had woken up lying beneath an ornate iron bridge that crossed a wide, sleepy river. A group of ducks paddled busily upstream in the dawn mist.

He shivered and gingerly felt the chill dampness of early morning dew on his clothes. Furtively, he crawled out from under the bridge and studied the landscape. One thing he immediately noticed was the absence of the giant two way tv screens. The other was a complete and blessed silence. Gone were the ever present strident voices urging the citizenry to Love Big Brother and Hate Emmanuel Goldstein.

He cowered under the bridge for another two hours until the sun rose, burning away the mist and warming the landscape. Then, gingerly, Winston emerged from his bolt hole and walked up the riverbank to join the road that led into a small nearby town. As he entered it, he froze. There towering in front of him was a giant television screen. It must have spotted him, but why hadn't the thought police appeared and arrested him? The chattering roar of a helicopter overhead was his answer.

Yes, here they come, he thought. But as he waited for the heavily armed automatons to jump from the aircraft and roughly grab him, nothing happened. Instead, the helicopter ignored him, passing overhead and clattering off into the distance.

There was also something distinctly odd about the telescreen. Instead of being filled with the baleful face of Big Brother, it was a swirling mass of colourful images. Out of this walked a tall and beautiful woman with her ebony skin draped in a diaphanous robe. In the background, instead of the repeated chant of *Big Brother! Big Brother!* a man's voice spoke with an odd gentleness:

"Amouage, the secret perfume of the ancients for the woman of tomorrow."

Winston Smith felt his whole being filled with an unfamiliar sensation that he had only experienced once in his life before. That was when he and Julia had furtively made love in the countryside within the shadow of that ruined church. It was the sensation of pure joy. No hatred, suspicion or fear just joy.

"Watch out you tosser! I nearly killed you." A lycra clad cyclist snarled at him as he whizzed by.

He had been so distracted, he had wandered into the traffic of the busy street. So many questions. How and why had the surveillance screens become so benign and what was a tosser?

Looking at the shops, he noticed their fronts were also filled with light, colour and joy. This was not the London or Airstrip One that he knew. That was a place filled with the drab, grey hatred of Big Brother. A place of fear and dread, of show trials where the corpses of class traitors dangled from gibbets, darkening the sky.

This sudden change left him feeling weak and disoriented. What was this? One of O'Brien's cruel tricks? He sat down heavily on a bench.

"Are you alright mister?" the girl sitting next to him asked, her young face etched with concern.

Strange, he thought, she was certainly young enough to be a member of the Hate League yet she had no sash. In fact her dress bore none of the hallmarks of the League: the regimental blouse and shapeless pants that concealed and denied the sexuality of the wearer.

"I can call an ambulance if you like," she said indicating the small device in her hand.

"What's that?" Winston asked in bafflement.

"You don't know what this is?"

He shook his head.

"You really don't know, do you?"

He shook his head again slowly

'It's a Smartphone dumbo. Everyone has 'em these days! You can't live without them. Look I've been texting my mate." The girl held the phone up to show Winston. He read the words on the screen:

Wot U fancy tonite babe? Purple Melon?

Rite on came the almost instant reply.

At last Winston Smith, reviser of history at The Ministry of Truth at Airstrip One in Oceania, found himself on familiar ground. He was reading Newspeak, the official language of 1984.

The girl could not help feeling sorry for this thin, haunted man next to her. Poor bugger, he really needed cheering up. Then she had an idea.

'Come on mate, I come with me. What did you say your name was?"

"Smith, Winston Smith."

And that was how they landed up in The Spotted Hen. Everything would have been fine if he had not tried to pay for the drinks. The woman behind the bar was sort of alright when he asked for a Victory Gin.

"Haven't heard of that one," she said. "Sipsmiths London Classic's popular though."

Winston agreed to give it a try. One mouthful told him why. It had a truly powerful kick, quite unlike the insipid liquid they served up at The Chestnut Tree. After rummaging around in his pockets, Winston pulled out some new dollars to pay for their drinks. The woman behind the bar frowned as she examined the money.

"No mate, you'll have to do better than this bloody monopoly money!" She said, slamming the coins back in his hand.

Winston only had a vague recollection of the argument that followed. Then what he assumed were the thought police turned up and took him away.

Better handle this one a bit carefully, Daly thought as he entered the interrogation room. You never know who you're picking up these days. Wasn't Howard Hughes arrested as a vagrant once?

"Right sir," Daly said, sitting down opposite Winston. "Let's start with your name and address shall we?"

"My name is Winston Smith."

"Address Winston?"

" Flat 2004, Fifth Floor, Victory Flats, Airstrip 1, Oceania.``

Daly suddenly had the uneasy feeling Winston was taking the Mickey out of him.

"Listen, Winston, we've been good and gentle with you so far, now don't spoil things mate. Just give me your address."

A look of genuine bafflement crept over Winston's face.

"But that *is* my address."

"So what's the date then?"

"11th May 1984."

"What are we going to do with him Sarge?" PC Foster asked him.

"Let him go I suppose, after all he hasn't actually committed any crimes has he?"

"He couldn't pay for his drink."

"If that was a criminal offence, our jails would all be permanently full."

"They are aren't they Sarge?"

' Alright cut the funny stuff Foster."

That confirmed it for Daly. This strange, thin man in overalls was obviously not the full ticket. He was living in an era forty years previously. He snapped his notebook shut and returned

151

to the interview suite.

"Right Winston, this is your lucky day. We've decided to release you with a caution. Just keep out of trouble in future."

As he led him out to the entrance, Daly thrust a couple of fivers in the man's overalls. Quite why he did that, he was not sure, except he felt sorry for this rather pathetic individual.

Winston Smith wandered down the street in a daze. He was completely adrift in a world very different from that of Airstrip One. He had found some similarities with the world of Big Brother, such as the tv screens and he was sure that young girl had been writing in Newspeak on that machine of hers.

With the late spring sun burning down on his overalls, he began to feel uncomfortably hot. Seeing the entrance of a pub called The Wishing Well he turned inside where an excitable man's voice seemed to fill the room. He saw it was coming from a large telescreen above the bar. A man and a woman with bright clothes covering their dark brown skins were watching it intently. Every so often, they would mutter something to one another in a language Smith did not understand.

Strange, he thought, they look like Eastasians. But if that's the case they are Oceania's enemies and we are at war with them. As the enemy, they should have been locked up or executed. Instead, they were obviously free.

"And tonight on Big Brother, we have four new contestants!"

Once again, Winston felt a surge of recognition. It was Big Brother!

"Big Brother, Big Brother," he began to chant at first quietly and then in a louder voice. "Big Brother, Big Brother, Big Brother!"

O'Brien was still chanting those two words when he awoke from that strange nightmare. Was it real? Had Winston Smith somehow managed to escape their clutches, never to be re-educated? No, it was not possible. Nobody ever escaped the thought police in Room 101.

WHEN BONEY INVADED BRITAIN

On a beautifully calm August day in 1798 three French frigates dropped their anchors in a remote Irish bay. Looking anxiously through his spyglass, General Jean Joseph Humbert scanned the shoreline for enemy troops, but it was empty of any threat.

"The weather and God are with us *Mon General*," murmured Lt August Borlet his Aide-de-camp.

"Not like Bantry," Humbert replied.

"No sir, that was a *grande catastrophe*, but this will be our victory over the English."

Both men vividly remembered the earlier expedition under General Hoche in 1796. Then the French had attempted to land at Bantry Bay in the far southwest of Ireland only to see their boats dashed to pieces in the surf and their men drown. That debacle was caused mainly by the worst winter weather in fifty years. Bitterly, Humbert remembered when the ship he was on *Le Droits de l'Homme* was sunk by a British frigate. He nearly drowned that day. This time he vowed, it would be different.

Eleven hundred French troops disembarked at Kilala Strand on that day, led by one of France's most promising generals. Thirty-one-year-old Humbert had rapidly risen through the ranks to become a brigadier general at the young age of 27. If anyone could see *Les Anglais* off it would be Humbert.

Striking south through the beautiful green and rocky Irish landscape, the French troops were joined by 1000 excitable local members of United Irishmen rebels waving their pitchforks and scythes. A few miles down the road, they came upon the local militia defending the town of Castlebar. In the brief battle that followed, the Franco-Irish forces put the local militia to flight in a crackle of musketry. That encounter would always be remembered as *The Castlebar Races*.

In the captured town, Humbert raised the flag of The Irish Republic - a golden harp against a green background to the wild cheers of the local populace. Then, mounted on a handsome grey horse, he led his growing force of French soldiers and rebels out towards the main prize of Dublin.

This initial skirmish in Ireland marked the start of the Napoleonic Invasion of Britain. In the pre-dawn darkness of the same day, the massive French invasion fleet of hundreds of barges moved out into the channel towards the English coast from a line of ports stretching down from Antwerp in the French-occupied Netherlands to St Malo and Rochfort in the South. Many were being towed by ships of the French Navy whilst others travelled under their own power. These vessels were driven partially by crude steam engines and partly by sail. Crammed on board were hundreds of troops of what Napoleon fondly called his *Armee d'Angleterre or Army of England.* With them were canon, siege engines and cavalry.

From the bridge of his flagship, *Duc d'Armagnac* freshly commissioned for this great venture, Emperor Napoleon Bonaparte observed the huge fleet move out of Calais Harbour with baited breath. Not more than a week earlier, the whole invasion had seemed on the verge of collapse when a trial run went disastrously wrong. A fault in the design of the flat-bottomed barges had rendered them unfit for landing on the English coast. A number of vessels had sunk with the loss of many men. However, the Emperor had kept his nerve and forced his shipwrights to work day and night on a redesign. Now the die was cast. If these favourable winds held, in a matter of days, London, the great prize, would be his. In his imagination, he saw himself being crowned Emperor of Europe from the throne of Westminster Abbey.

Not for the first or last time, the British spy network, such as it was, had let down its military masters. The British Government had, of course, been aware of the massive build-up of Napoleonic forces in Channel ports such as Calais, Cherbourg and Dunkirk. But their agents in France had assured them that the invasion force would not be ready for weeks. The trouble was, most of these harbingers of good news were double agents in the pay of Napoleon *"The Great Disturber"*. So, on that balmy summer's morning in late August 1798, the Royal Navy were caught napping.

There was only a skeleton patrol of frigates, not more than

five ships out in the Channel to challenge the French invasion fleet. The Admiralty had very unwisely relaxed the blockades of the French naval forces at Brest and Toulon under Collingwood and Nelson. Why they had done this was down to a mixture of ignorance of military strategy and complacency by their Lordships running the Admiralty. It was certainly contrary to the advice given by those two commanders of the blockades.

This allowed a mass break out of French warships who were then tasked by Napoleon to attack Dublin, Devonport and Portsmouth in lightning raids. The endgame was to fire these ports and destroy the Royal Navy ships anchored there. It was a bold stroke typical of Napoleon. "Let us be masters of the Channel for six hours and we are masters of the World!" he had told his generals. Now, through British negligence, his plan looked to be reaching fruition.

As the sun appeared over the horizon at just before six in the morning, the watch high in the masts of *HMS Redoubt* stationed just off Spithead, was the first to see the massive invasion fleet baring down on them. No sooner had he been notified, Captain Harry Vaux, ordered the *Redoubt* to battle stations. As the frigate sailed at speed towards the barges and their escorts, she fired her first broadside. Two of the barges were hit with canon balls and grapeshot tearing into their infrastructure. The casualties amongst the tightly packed troops were extensive and bloody. On one of the barges, a large brazier was hit sending a deadly shower of burning embers across its deck.

The wooden vessel soon caught fire and within minutes the barge was ablaze. In the fiery chaos, all order broke down as men and horses fought to escape the vessel. Not more than five minutes later the barge erupted in a deadly orange flower of fire as the flames reached its powder store. Now, almost torn in two, the great barge listed sharply as she began to sink. The crew of the *Redoubt* could hear the dreadful cries of hundreds of men as the burning pyre of the barge sank beneath the waves.

Not that the British ship had any time for leisurely contemplation. No sooner had she attacked the barges, than two of the French warships broke off and attacked her on both sides. What followed was one of many fierce naval engagements on that day. With her superior and highly trained gun crews, *Redoubt* poured shot into the two French ships at close range. However, their combined firepower ultimately proved too great for the brave little ship and *HMS Redoubt* was demasted. Meanwhile, the rest of the invasion force pressed on towards the English Beaches.

All along the South Coast of England watch-outs in Martello towers and other observation points were waking up to the terrible reality of a French invasion. Militias were already pouring, sleepy eyed out of barracks from Harwich to Plymouth. They would take up defensive positions on roads and at the edge of towns, villages and cities to repel the French hordes. By eight o'clock the land was filled with the sounds of church bells ringing. They carried one message:

"Invasion! Invasion!" They seemed to cry, "Englishmen defend your land against the barbaric gallic hordes! May God be with you."

Of course, he was! Just as he was with the French taking the Holy Sacrament as they waited to pour onto the beaches.

Along the clifftops of Southern England beacons lit up to spread word of the invasion.

In London, Prime Minister William Pitt the Younger had been awakened in the early hours by a breathless messenger with the news of the invasion. After sending out runners to inform his cabinet, he went post haste in a carriage to King George III's residence at Kew Palace to give the monarch the dreadful news.

The King was outraged as was Pitt by the fact that Napoleon had stolen a march on them.

"God's blood Mr Pitt, how could this be allowed to happen?" George fumed. "Damee! We have the strongest, nay the best Navy in the world and the Frenchies are walking all over us!"

"Your Majesty, there will be a full reckoning for this failure I can assure you," Pitt replied. "But now we must decide the best course of action."

It was quickly agreed by the Pitt Cabinet and the military

leaders that the government would leave London for Weedon in Northamptonshire. The large Royal Ordnance Depot there was already being prepared to accommodate the Government and Military High Command in the event of a Napoleonic Invasion.

George III was a good and patriotic King who was horrified by "this act of cowardice". He wanted to "stand my ground and face Boney" as he put it by staying in London. It was only after much persuasion and cajoling by Pitt, other advisors and his wife Charlotte that he agreed to go along with the idea.

As the morning progressed, the carriages carrying cabinet ministers and their families along with the Royal Family sped out of London on the Great North Road. They were passed in the opposite direction by troops pouring in to defend the capital. Manning all the bridges, streets and cross roads were members of the trained bands and the City's own Regiment, The Honourable Artillery Company. Commanding them was the former Lord Mayor and well respected City luminary Sir William Curtis MP.

By eight o'clock, many troops of the French Invasion were landing on various beaches up and down the South Coast. The two hundred thousand strong *Armee d'Angleterre* was pouring ashore and preparing to move inland towards the towns and cities in the heart of England.

The first major engagement with invaders on English soil occurred just before nine o'clock in the Romney Marsh in Kent. As a large force of French troops and mounted cuirassiers moved across the wetland, they were already being slowed down by the many drainage channels and waterways that ran across this otherwise flat landscape.

Half a mile short of the town of Rye, the French forces encountered a mixed British force of militia and regular troops who had been garrisoned there. Their Commander, Captain Vaisey-Stuart ordered the men to spread out in the coppices, bushes and hedgerows scattered across the marshes. The first the French knew of this threat was an intense volley of musketry that tore their advancing front line to shreds. Their cavalry found they could not charge across this broken treacherous terrain as they would in the flat European plains. Because of this, their usefulness was greatly blunted. The Battle of Romney Marsh lasted an hour and a half during which time a larger French Force of fifteen hundred men were scattered and driven back by four hundred British musketeers. In the end, it was the defenders who held the field in what was a legendary feat of arms.

Meanwhile, the main part of the invasion force was besieging Dover and Chatham under the overall command of Admiral Étienne Eustache Bruix, Napoleon's Navy Minister. Dover was extremely well fortified and proved to be too hard a nut to crack. Bruix directed his forces to bypass the port and strike north toward Canterbury.

By mid-afternoon, the Napoleonic Forces had moved twenty miles inland. Progress had been much slower than anticipated due to the difficult countryside of hedgerows, walls, fencing and drainage ditches. Added to this, were the increasing numbers of British troops they were having to fight. Now the initial shock of the invasion had worn off, the British armed forces were becoming more organised and providing serious opposition to the advancing *Armee d'Anglais*. The French were also fast realising another inconvenient truth. With 600,000 men the British outnumbered their invasion force by three to one.

As night fell, the situation remained confused. Major sea battles had occurred off Gravesend, Chatham, Portsmouth and Devonport. In them, both sides had lost ships. Harwich was largely on fire and the British had been routed in The Battle of Canterbury. As yet neither side had managed to seize a crucial initiative that would win the day.

However, Napoleon still believed he could conquer England since he possessed a vital secret weapon which would bring him victory. Since dawn, a silent armada of balloons had been launched from the French mainland ten miles from the Channel coast. Under the command of Marie Madeline Sophie Blanchard a brilliant early aeronaut, over one hundred balloons full of troops floated over the coast towards England. Provided the winds remained favourable, the balloons would drift far into the English countryside. There they could land and the disembarking troops would cut off the British forces from the rear. For good measure, the balloons also carried bombardiers. These were specialist soldiers who would drop crude bombs on British towns and cities. Their weapons were little more than bottles with a lighted fuse and filled with gunpowder and brandy. Nevertheless, they were deadly and effective for all that.

"I will set England ablaze," Blanchard had promised Napoleon.

The success or failure of a great military operation often hinges on a small event that has a disproportionate effect on the outcome. In the case of The Napoleonic Invasion of England, it was down to what some wag had dubbed her unpredictable weather as *General Nature*. At one o'clock in the morning of the second day, the winds changed by 180 degrees.

Suddenly, Blanchard found her balloons were no longer about to cross the white cliffs of Dover but were being driven inexorably back towards the French mainland. At the same time, a bank of dark clouds blew in across the country, drenching the land in heavy rain. Many of the French forces found themselves bogged down in a quagmire of mud, effectively bringing their advance to a halt.

Caught up in a fierce thunderstorm, many of Blanchard's balloons were destroyed by lightning strikes. In the darkness lit only by lightning flashes, she watched in horror as one flaming balloon after the other fell into the sea spilling out fiery human figures. It was only by some miracle, that her balloon made it back to Paris and safety.

At sea, both Admiral Collingwood and Nelson had managed to get a significant number of their ships out of various ports. This enabled them to sail round to the rear of the invading barges cutting them off from their supply vessels. Many of these and their escorting ships were attacked and sunk in numerous fierce and savage mini-battles.

By the fourth day, the combined forces of the weather and a larger British Force had fought Napoleon's *Armee Anglais* to a halt. Its commander, Admiral Etienne Bruix had to sue for peace. Over the next week or so, the shattered remnants of the invading French Army returned shamefacedly to their homeland.

Perhaps the bitterest blow was suffered by Napoleon whose dearest ambition was to be crowned Emperor of all Europe from the throne in Westminster Abbey. This had now been thwarted for all time.

About The Author

Nick Brazil in The Greyhound, his local pub with his dog Harold.

Nick Brazil is an author, film maker, photographer and public speaker. He was born in Looe, Cornwall and now lives in a Thameside village in Oxfordshire, England. He has travelled and worked extensively in Southern Africa, Europe, The Middle East and America. In 1991, he travelled with a small charity to Albania when it was transitioning from an isolationist communist state to democracy. He described that trip as a journey through a state of anarchy which included encounters with gun-waving secret police. *The Ambush Was Closed for Lunch* is his sixth book.

Printed in Great Britain
by Amazon